THE TRIAL OF AGENT WHITEHALL

ALSO BY STEVEN RICHARD SMITH

King of Methamphetamine Valley

The Honest Applicant

The Accidental Girlfriend

THE TRIAL OF
AGENT WHITEHALL

Steven Richard Smith

Maybe I love fear. The danger out here on the edge.
Maybe I'm afraid of love. A soft bed I'll never leave.

—Ray McNiece

CHAPTER ONE

I just killed a man. The chrome door of the casino elevator rolled open. "Whoa!" I shouted, swinging an arm around Liz. Beneath the light of the elevator car, a large figure appeared, a second at his shoulder. Both wore leather vests and tangled beards. Large meaty men with twisted faces stepped off.

"Whoa?" the first one echoed. "Whoa what?" He squinted at me and ambled toward the lights and bells of the casino.

"Aw, nothing," I said, shaking my head. "I thought you were somebody else." I sighed and motioned Liz into the car. Gerard wheeled the baggage cart onto the elevator.

"You got some ghosts," the second biker said.

I called to them, "Yeah, I guess I do." Before stepping in, I noticed the moniker Fugitives M.C. embroidered on their vests, broken leg irons unfurled across the middle of their backs. The second biker twisted his neck at me as they went, his lips murmuring.

The elevator door floated to a close and Liz slid next to me. My good hand trembled at her shoulder.

"I know what you were thinking," she whispered, her eyes fixed on the LED plate. Its numbers clicked upward.

"Scared the shit out of me," I said.

She took my hand. "It's okay now."

Gerard studied us, his fingers wrapped around the frame of the cart. "Sir, can I get you anything for that," he said, tipping his chin toward the hand that dangled free, "for your hand there?"

The elevator tinkled a melodic faint bell at each floor. "Your guy at the front desk already asked me. I appreciate it. But I'll tell you what: I could use some gauze and tape, maybe some ointment. You guys got a first aid kit somewhere?"

Gerard brushed something from his shoulder and made a slight sucking noise with his teeth. "Do we. We got a full-time nurse on staff downstairs. She's always around, paid to help any guest who needs medical attention. Would you like me to send her up, sir?" Gerard's black hair tufted along his rather large head, his age reflecting, I guessed, 35 years.

I looked at Liz, she winced back. "You probably should, huh?"

"I was just going to soak it," I said with a shrug. The car ballooned to a slow stop and the chrome doors opened. The top floor just smelled posh, wall-to-wall thick carpeting, wall tiles following imperial patterns down the hallway.

"She could at least take a look at it," Liz said, stepping into the quiet corridor.

"Yeah, I guess so."

Gerard led us to the hallway's end, where French doors opened inward to a massive suite. In the center of the room, a gargantuan bed crowned by a canopy was laden with fluffy bedding; no fewer than a dozen throw pillows of zigzag design capped off the hallway décor.

"Oh, look at this place," Liz said. The cart stalled behind her and Gerard strolled around the room, flipping switches that rained dimmed beacons, casting shadows over upholstered mahogany chairs and an overstuffed divan angled in the corner. Liz disappeared into the bathroom though I could hear her oohs and ahs. "Oh, look at that," she gushed.

I smiled and collapsed into the luxury of an expansive chair, unlacing a shoe. Gerard opened doors to the armoire, which revealed a television with a screen no smaller than a kitchen table. "These counters are marble," Liz called out.

Gerard looked at me as I flipped a shoe from my foot. I smiled at what she'd said and he nodded. "The ladies always fancy the bathrooms in the suite."

"I can see that." Within minutes, he had placed the bags about the room, and set the blinds to filter out the red and blue glow of the Strip below. At my feet I set the crockpot box and rubbed my toes into the thick carpeting.

"Sir, I'll have the nurse up soon," he said, wheeling the cart from the room and gliding the doors to a vacuumed click. I had considered peeling off a tip but remembered handing him ten dollars at the front desk. The lights in the bathroom went dark and Liz walked back in on silent feet.

"He's gone," I said.

"You're tired, huh?"

I slumped down and loosened the other shoe as she reached toward the ceiling with a yawn then tugged at the sleeve of her sweater.

"Yeah," I mused, "and to think I had plans for us to gamble tonight."

"How about the desk clerk thinking we had a real crockpot in the box?" she joked.

I nodded. "I caught that. He probably would have flipped out if you would've opened it up and shown him the money."

"I mean, there are probably millionaires in here all the time, but eighty grand is like a million to me," she said. "It's always been a one-dollar tip at a time for me."

A bare elbow flitted beneath her shirt and in a flash, a nude shoulder shone under the amber light as I sat watching. Though we'd been together several times, the sight of her breasts, jiggling beneath a black bra, struck me. She moved about, completely uninhibited, looping the sweater's neck above her head.

"Boy, do you look good," I hummed from the chair, "even after all we've been through tonight. You'd never know by looking at you that we just . . ."

She threw her head back and scrunched her nose with a crooked smile. "That's a nice compliment, but this thing is going in the trash," she said, rolling the sweater into a ball and reaching for a brass wastebasket. "It's covered in tiny pieces of glass." When she shot an arm behind her and unsnapped the bra, it left pink impressions across her back. Her firm breasts ebbed a bit and I imagined my hands cupped along them.

"The nurse is going to be up here soon," I said.

"She's seen other women, I'm sure of it," Liz scoffed with a roll of her eyes. She padded toward her bag on the chiffonier.

When I first heard distant footsteps in the hallway, I remembered the shooting and sprang to my feet and threw the deadbolt. Seconds later the bell rang, a tier of descending chimes that resonated throughout the room. I peered through the peephole, expecting to see a haggard woman in a blue frock, her hair jerked back in a meaningless bobble, a midnight soul established as the one to inflict pain on infirmed guests. Instead, I opened the door to an attractive nurse. A real nurse, waves of brunette hair pinned beneath a cap. Dressed head to toe in white, she wore a tag that identified her as an employee of the casino, though I might have imagined myself in a hospital—or a dream.

"Mr. Butler? Gary Butler?" she asked.

I blushed, noticing the medical bag at the end of her arm. "Yeah, that's me."

"I'm Cynthia, the hotel nurse on duty tonight. Mr. Simmons, the desk clerk, said you might need medical attention. Do you mind if I come in and take a look at that hand?" Her voice was warm but her brown eyes were all business. I turned and signaled toward the bright lights of the bathroom. In the corner of the room, Liz rummaged through her bags and threw a careless wave at the woman. *And this is my topless girlfriend Liz.*

A row of vanity globes burned, bright fluorescence straining my tired eyes. At the counter she set down her bag and snapped it open.

"I realize it's late and that you're probably tired but I have a medical registration form I'm going to need filled out." A small cardstock form appeared on the counter. A pen clicked in her hand.

I sighed, "Oh, no kidding." I held up my hand. "Well, if I can write with this, we'll be okay." I slid the form close and my fingers shrank around the pen with pain. "Okay, 'name' . . . and Gary Butler. Got that. 'Age' Twenty-five. 'Other persons in your party'? Oh, that's her. Leslie "Liz" Smith. 'Existing Medical Conditions'

None. 'Allergies' None. 'Reason for Treatment' Cut hand, I'll put. And signing here and 'date'? What is the date? I forgot."

"The twenty-third," she whispered.

"Right. May 23rd, 1990. And here you go." I returned the pen and card and she whirled toward her bag.

"Now I understand we have a laceration to the left hand? Is that correct? You can just sit here in this chair, if you would," she said with a tap of her fingers. "Are you favoring one ankle?"

"Yeah, I sprained it but was just about to make an ice bag for it. It's not too bad, actually."

"That'll take the swelling down. I can look at it once I'm done with your hand, if you'd like."

I plopped down near the sink with a sigh, offering up my limp left arm. I unfolded my hand, its bandage creased with moist dirt. "Yeah, we were changing out a window before we left this morning when I, uh, fell backwards. Not a very good way to start a vacation, I know."

"Mm hmm, let's take a look at your hand," she said, her tone motherly. She moved her hips into the half-circle of my arm, so I dropped my head away from her, detaching myself from the limb and her backside. As she unraveled the bandage, I felt air rush to the wound and her eyes scrutinizing it. "Well, you've got a fairly good sized sliver still in there. Can you feel it?"

"Uh huh," I grunted, trying not to consider the piece of glass in my body. "What, you probably get old timers with heart attacks in this place, don't you?"

Her fingers dabbed at my palm. "Sometimes. We do have our share of patrons, as you might expect, overeating then, what, with the stresses of gambling—"

"I feel that," I announced. A cold metal instrument pressed against my palm, sharpening the pain to a rolling sensation through the wrist.

"Almost . . . got it, Mr. Butler. Oh." Her breathing halted and she sighed. "Okay, here's what I need: I need you to be very still for me. There it is . . . it's coming."

Cynthia braced my arm by planting her hips into my shoulder, all of her energy poised at removing the glass. Liz appeared in the doorway. Her brow furrowed. I raised my eyebrows as if to joke, 'hey, look at me.' My face was near the small of Cynthia's back, enough for Liz to get the wrong idea. Liz froze, standing there in a plush white robe, Bally's embroidered on it. Liz shifted to my right side and gathered my good hand in hers, looking in my eyes as the nurse remained hunched over my other hand. For a second, I considered the scene, being treated by this bombshell nurse, my beautiful girlfriend cradling my other hand. I grinned and whispered to Liz, "This is a lot better than being at the cabin."

"You behave," she scolded and squeezed my fingers.

"And that is that," Cynthia exclaimed, a pair of tweezers in her fingers raised to the ceiling light. "That had to be painful while lodged in your hand like that, Mr. Butler."

"Yeah," I said, "it didn't feel good, that's for sure."

Liz looked down at me and mouthed *Mr. Butler?* I raised my eyebrows back at her with a tilt of my head at the nurse.

There was a small clatter at the marble counter as Cynthia rummaged through her bag. "Now, we'll just clean this up and get a dressing on it."

Liz made a mocking face behind the nurse, tipping her head side to side and making her lips clap as a puppet's. I almost laughed. When Liz saw me grin, she stepped back, her eyes fixed on the nurse who splashed hot, painful water over the wound. Gripping either side of her robe, Liz flashed her nude body at me. I dropped my head to the floor to stifle my laughter, shaking my head for her to stop.

"Honey, could you look for my clothes out there while she finishes up?"

"Sure, dear," Liz said and made a playful face. She disappeared.

"You two here on a honeymoon?" Cynthia asked as she applied some kind of medicated cream and then bundled my hand in gauze. The circumference of my hand was covered in a doubled band of tape.

"Nah, just boyfriend-girlfriend getting away to do a little gambling, you know." I had noticed her perfume when she walked in, patchouli.

"Ah. Well, I'm leaving you this tube of topical cream. Your wound could use a stitch or two, but you should be okay if you keep it clean. Either way, you will have a little scar tissue once your hand heals. Give it some time and let the air get to it once you see it beginning to close up." She gave my ankle a cursory exam. "With ice and these ibuprofen, you should be okay. Just try to keep your weight off it while it heals."

"That shouldn't be a problem. Thanks for everything."

As she gathered her things from the counter and washed up, I went to my pocket for a larger bill. She noticed and waved a hand. I realized that she was my height, a slim woman, symmetrical. "I'm sorry, Mr. Butler. The hotel doesn't allow us to accept tips. We're compensated by the casino as a service to its guests." She sounded like a robot.

The twenty dollar bill hung from my fingertips as I thought of something to say. "Ah, I get it. If you did it for tips, you might just go around fixing up people that aren't even sick, huh?" It was a clumsy thing to say. "I mean, you wouldn't do that, though. With the oath and all, I mean."

She smiled, her eyes seeking a way out, and moved past me for the doorway.

"Well, thank you very much, Cynthia. I really do appreciate it," I said, holding my bandaged hand at her. "Feels better already."

"You're welcome. Have a good night, Mr. Butler."

"Thank you. You, too," I said, allowing the door to fall to a close. I locked it. Behind me, Liz was spread out beneath the canopy, her eyes watchful.

"Have a good night, Mr. Butler," she mocked in a husky voice. "I'll be back to take care of you later, Mr. Butler."

"You know, you never struck me as the jealous kind," I said.

She smirked and pursed her lips. "How come you gave her my first name but not my last?"

"Because I did the same with my own. I didn't want to slip and call you by your first name, either. Now if they come looking for us, they can't identify us. We're just Mr. Butler and Miss Smith of Cleveland, Ohio. See?"

She nodded and I smiled as I went to draw the bath. After some time of sloshing around with Liz in the Jacuzzi, I eased my head back with the jets running. That's when I dozed off.

There was a discreet tapping at the door. "Room service," someone offered.

"Our steaks," I said, splashing from the tub and leaving pools of water on the floor.

"Ooh, baby," Liz teased as I wrapped myself in a robe and trotted for the door. A cart of steaming food squealed into the room, and I paid the man. Once toweled off and in shorts and shirts for the night, we ate to our fill, our eyes puffed for sleep. Liz peeled back the covers. I went around the room, killing the overhead lights Gerard had set, and drew the blinds flush. Within a few minutes, I was under the blankets and next to her body, the sweep of her back familiar to my hands, her hair shampooed and damp near my face. Within minutes, Liz was sleeping. I rolled to my back with a sigh, my hand resting on my belly. That was all I remembered.

CHAPTER TWO

The desert sun was at half-mast, cleared of a bleached horizon. Panes of hot light blanketed the eastern faces of casinos making up the skyline. As I turned the blinds, natural light fell across the room and I sat back in a heavy chair and rested my feet on its stuffed ottoman. My ankle was stiff and my hand smarted, a bee sting sensation that refused to go away. Liz slept, her hair golden-skipped in strands across her cheek. I yawned at the ransacked luggage, unzipped, with yesterday's clothes strewn across the floor in spots. At the cart I gnawed at a large scrap of steak she'd discarded and thought to take the aspirin left on the bathroom counter.

Fresh images from the cabin shooting scrolled through my mind. I shuddered at the reconstructed scene. Those guys had tried to kill us, driving up there with the sole intent of murdering us both. I imagined what hateful spirit had driven them, their necessary discussions along the way: who was carrying what pistol, how much ammunition they had, and most of all, how much Gorman wanted to kill me. What had he called me, *ATF*? Not even a person by name but an agency. I was that faceless to him. The notion of the shootings sickened me even though it was over. What if I'd been weak, a man with no instinct for survival?

I had to snap out of this. Gorman was dead. I had killed him. And I had killed his best friend. I had committed a double murder. How did that sound? How could I ever put words to it, explain to loved ones what I'd done? Murders were the stuff of Hollywood, not something you have to bury.

My hand radiated pain and I was lost to the nightmare again, a sheen of sweat on my face. I shook it off, got up, and limped around the room for something to do—anything. The brooding, I knew, would come fresh every morning from this day forward. *I had killed a man.* I took a deep breath and let it out with a hiss. I knelt where clothes were strewn and rubbed with gentle fingers the bandage. Then I looked up at Liz sleeping. I felt sick. The Elton John song about killing a king scrolled through my mind and . . . Liz stirred. She rolled over facing me and blinked. I raised an Indian chief's hand at her. She lie there, the first smile of the day.

"Good morning. How'd you sleep?"

"Good," she answered, pushing back errant hair with a stretch of her arms. She sat upright and studied the room. "What time is it?"

"It's time for breakfast," I said, leaning forward to spot the LED clock I'd noticed in the night when I'd stumbled to the bathroom. "It's just after nine."

"Nine," she sniffed, "we slept that late? Gosh."

"I know, I feel good. I feel like a rock star. And to think that before we left California I'd pictured we'd get here last night and hit the slots. Boy, how strange that seems now."

"Gambling?" She yawned again and clamped her lips. "You serious?"

"Mm, just some slots. I thought it'd be fun."

"Hmm." She swung her legs off the bed and stood, her loose night shirt falling over her in waves. A teddy bear cartooned in white and yellow rolled across her chest.

"Nice teddy."

Liz pattered around the bed with her arms spreading open for me as I met her there. "Hmmm," she whispered, "I feel like a new person."

"I wish I did."

"What's that mean?"

"Ah, nothing. Forget it," I said. She pulled away and rifled through her bag for something to wear, and I found laundered jeans and a t-shirt, Neil Young emblazoned above a field of wheat stalks and a distant sun. We were off for breakfast, pulling and tugging at one another like moony teenagers on the elevator while Harold and Marge from Kansas crowded in with their cumbersome baggage. The two of them were dabbed with suntan lotion, a roadmap in his fingers, sunglasses hanging from her neck. They both studied the elevator light as it changed. Liz made eyes at me and I clutched, as a boxed football, our crockpot.

In the restaurant a rail-thin waitress, who reminded Liz of the cat-eyed woman from the Village Inn, scribbled our orders on a pad: lobster tails and a large OJ. A steak and hash browns, coffee black.

"I can't believe this breakfast," she marveled once it arrived. "It's so cheap," she said, fluttering a napkin across her lap.

I looked around at the vibrant scene, rows and rows of slot machines. "That's because they want you to gamble. You know something? We could play slots this morning, if you want." The bells and lights of machines pulsed and rang. The breakfast crowd had dwindled to a few older couples sipping coffee.

Liz frowned and shook her head as she speared and dug at the lobster.

"What?"

She leaned in. "I just don't think we should waste our money on that. You know we'll lose. Besides, I thought the rule was we'd use it for something good."

"Right you are. Boy, now I feel bad," I chuckled and dipped a forkful of hash browns in ketchup.

"It's okay," she said and patted my bandaged hand. "I thought the money we spent at that all-night gas station was good."

"No kidding. I thought for sure we were going to run out."

"How's your hand, by the way?"

"It still hurts a little. But it'll be fine," I said and scissored the rare steak and grinned at Liz. I felt better having her there with me and had a pleasant, bubbled feeling about the day ahead of us. The casino's repetitive tunes and ringing bells reminded me of a cash register that's totaling up an endless transaction, annoying in its flash of mustard lights and jingling peals. I leaned over to keep my comment private. "You know, something hit me this morning. I was upstairs at the window, looking over the city in its first light. It reminded me of waking up next to Robin after she'd been drunk out of her mind in Fresno. I don't know why I remembered that. You know, some of us love the sobriety of morning. It wakes up people that need to be hit with bright light. She'd be perfect for this town, though, drunk all the time."

"It's going to take some time—for both of us—to leave that whole Valley scene behind."

"Tell me about it." Raising the tines of my fork, I whispered, "It dawned on me that if somebody asked me this morning, 'hey, what'd you do last night?' I'd have to say in all truth, I killed two people."

"Don't do that to yourself," she said. "Don't. You saved our lives. Had the circumstances been different for us, the newspapers would be interviewing you this morning, calling you a hero."

I slumped my shoulders and rested the fork. "I still feel bad," I sighed, "I never wanted to kill anybody or anything, not even a chipmunk as a kid. And now I can't take it back." My head rested in my palms. "Oh, God, just listen to that. *I killed someone.*"

The skinny waitress's shoes appeared at the floor where I was staring. "Sir, is your breakfast okay?"

I sensed Liz nodding at her. "He's fine. We just had some bad news this morning, is all."

"Well, I hope nothing serious."

"No, no. Thank you, though, for asking. And whenever you have a minute, we'll take our check."

"Oh, sure." I heard footsteps moving away as I dabbed my face with the napkin spread on my lap.

"I'm sorry about this," I choked, rearing back in my chair, reluctant to look around the place for curious faces that might have noticed me.

"Don't be. You're goodhearted. It's what I love about you," she whispered, "like the night you stood up for that old lady."

I cleared my throat and sat up straight, rubbing my chest with a rolling shrug. I looked around again. "Yeah, I'll be fine," I said between rigid lips.

Just then, Liz smiled at me, her blonde hair pulled from her face and clipped. "Look on the bright side. What happened, even though it was terrible, has made us that much closer." Distant sunlight broke across the room and shone through her eyes. With her I felt human again.

* * *

With our bags loaded and the map on my knee, I sat in the car and traced the lines from Vegas to Flagstaff. With her passenger door flung open, Liz settled two coffee cups between the bucket seats. The air was cool, dry as stone. Traffic streaked along nearby streets. We shot down Las Vegas Boulevard, looking for the freeway that would carry us toward Henderson. We climbed into the mountains and buzzed around Lake Mead, its water sky blue and primitive.

A short time later, the Honda rolled into Arizona. Strands of hair whipped around Leslie's cheeks once I opened the roof. I'd plotted Nevada into Arizona and three hours beyond the state line. A town called Dolan Springs lay paper flat along the isolated highway. The traffic thinned, and we passed a large sedan, cinnamon-purple. It took me back to the black death-car, and I remembered how its doors were thrown open and how the two figures had galloped toward the cabin. Last night. Flashing before my eyes, red fire roared from the barrel's end and a dark figure lay crumpled in the dirt.

"Are you okay?" Liz's voice broke my concentration.

"Uh, yeah."

"Something was bothering you just now. I could tell."

I shrugged and chewed on a toothpick to where its end had splintered. "It was. I was thinking about you know what."

"You're going to need to let that go. It's behind us now," she said, a flatness to her voice.

I squinted at the vast stone rising in the distance. "It's not that easy, though. I got the feeling this morning that this thing's going to be with me for a while. For life maybe, I don't know." The car hummed along the road, the desert valley stretched out yawning, much wider than California's High Desert.

"Just give it time. It'll work out. We knew there would be costs going in, right?"

"I guess. You know that actor who plays Bubba in *In the Heat of the Night*?"

"Yeah, I love that show," she said.

"Really? I would not have guessed it. Well, anyway, I used to see that Bubba guy at the gym in Fresno. It's not important, but I used to watch the show. I swear, there'd be a murder on it every week. If you noticed, the population of the town—what is it, Sparta? The population's six hundred or something. I always joked with Robin that the show could never last because every week someone gets killed. Eventually you'd have no cast members left, except maybe Carroll O'Connor."

"That's true. There are a lot of killings on it. I never thought about it like that. But what's that got to do with you?" She pulled back strands of hair, and then I felt her hand rest on my leg.

"I was just thinking," I sighed, "what happened last night was no TV program. We can't just turn it off and go to bed. I can't be that actor from the gym and just shrug off what happens on a Hollywood set. Our thing is reality. Right now, I mean, I could be wanted for murder."

She rode along blinking at me, the hum of the motor constant.

"You know?" I asked, a hint of demand in my voice.

She tipped her head and gazed out the window. "You think that's what they'll do? Come after us?"

I squeezed my cut hand into a ball to test it for pain. "I don't know. We acted in self-defense, right? So, you left your job and your boyfriend, big deal. There's nothing illegal about it. I resigned from ATF with a written notice and turned in all my equipment, so I don't think they can come after me for that, either."

She winced a little. "But we took money that wasn't ours, and we did break into that cabin."

"Yeah, but we also left cash to pay for the damages. I mean, yeah, they could string together a series of minor charges against us, but the drug money? How could police follow-up on that? Especially if it was never reported. Stan screamed that he knew we took it, but who's going to report us? The Red Hawks? They're not going to do that. That loss is a cost of doing business on the street. There are black market rip-offs all the time between dealers and gangs."

Liz rode a long time in silence. The sun grew warmer. I thought about popping in a tape to shake the mood. "Is that what we are?" she asked. "Crooks?"

"Of course not," I said, patting her hand, "don't be silly. But when someone's shot and dies from a bullet wound? Ah, I know one thing. Whoever did the shooting has to answer for it. That part I do know."

"Well, that's just great," she said.

"I think we should just go ahead with our plans, though, and see what happens, you know? Who knows, maybe they'll write it off as justice served. That's how it should go. I mean, come on, Stan was going away for 15 years with the new charges. That meant no chance for parole or anything. Just think about it. How people are always complaining about tax dollars spent to house criminals. It's not as though Stan learned anything with his recidivism being what it is."

"His what?" she giggled. She allowed her arm to dangle from the window, forming an airplane wing with her flattened hand.

"Recidivism. It means how many times you keep getting in trouble. Prison's supposed to teach convicts a lesson, so magically, they'll never want to return. All of that amounts to a bunch of social feel-good bullshit I learned in college." I grinned and scanned the highway.

"Oh, yeah," she said, "Stan really learned his lesson. Please."

The tachometer was steady as I glanced at the fuel gauge: Over three-quarters. "Well, maybe that's how the courts will see it. That the two of us did society a favor."

"What's this 'we' stuff, big guy? You're the one who did the shooting," she said in a taunting voice.

"Whoa. Who was on the floor yelling, 'shoot him, shoot him'?"

"You pulled the trigger and you know it," she tittered, her voice accusatory.

"Don't you feel bad?" I said, raising my voice. I reset my grip on the wheel and glared at her.

She nodded and rode in silence before speaking. "Of course, I feel bad. Maybe we shouldn't joke about it. Seriously. There's a lot about him I'm leaving behind, things that make me sick. And other things that died with him at that cabin. I decided this morning some things don't need sharing. Things I want to forget. You understand?"

"Uh huh." I swallowed.

"Gary, you didn't kill a man back there, so just stop it. You freed me from a prison. I got a second chance at life thanks to you. I was getting dressed this morning and kept thinking how much I respect you for that. Face the facts: There were two of them and one of you, and they had those pistols and you just had that—what'd you call it, 'a boy's shotgun'?

"I haven't had a chance to tell you this but I was relieved when I saw Stan lying dead out there. Really I was." Her eyes measured the road. "So, to answer your question about feeling bad—not at all. Not one bit, and no one's going to tell me I should feel bad, either." Her voice was slate, a gray sound. "You shot a human monster. Why don't you just feel good about that?"

"Well, since you put it that way," I said. My imagination was already miles away from her compliment, picturing instead Stanley, the son of hell, pinning her down and abusing her with his pants down. "I guess I should feel good about it. If I was sent to fight against Noriega and shot a soldier from Panama, I'd be justified.

"Or let's say I shot Stanley during the raid at the house when he made a sudden move and got Stubbs all fired up. I'd feel better about it. I guess I'm just hung up because the shootings happened outside the law."

Liz fell silent again, her wrist hung over the window's edge, her face stewing. She leaned forward and rummaged through her day bag, slipping an oversized pair of sunglasses out of it. We rode awhile more in silence. Her mouth wrinkled with emotion. "He used to beat me."

"You're kidding me," I said. "You know, honestly, I kind of figured that with some of the stuff you said."

"Because I wouldn't have sex with him," she bawled, "and he used to threaten to kill me if I ever tried to leave. Even my dad was afraid of him."

I let the car coast to a stop on the shoulder. We were stopped in front of an Arizona state road sign, 93. She was toweling her cheek with her hand. I put the car in park and was around the hood in a flurry of steps. I opened her door and knelt there. She turned and discarded the glasses, her face red with tears. I leaned in and Liz fell against my shoulder. "You were my way out, you were," she sobbed.

"It's going to be okay. He's dead. And now we got each other. Okay?" I braced her arms and nodded at her.

She sniffed, "Thanks."

* * *

As we rolled forward, it dawned on me that in this expansive valley we were one of only two motorists. I began gaining on a small silver Honda. Its female driver appeared to be enjoying the day, lengthy strands of hair being whipped around the car's interior. I kept back on her shoulder in the blind spot, a little anxious to pass. Our car hummed forward, evening to her rate of speed. Side-by-side racing, we knifed toward a mountain canyon. The blonde held fast to her wheel with athletic arms. I guessed her a volleyball player from the California coast leaving Las Vegas. She looked over and smiled. I raised my open fingers in a wave and passed.

"Oh, she's flirting with you," Liz teased. Her face had dried.

"Yeah, right, except there's one problem with that."

"What's that?"

"I already got a girl."

"Oh," she cried, "you are so conceited. She doesn't like you."

"Man, you're cold-blooded." Then I burst out laughing and she tickled me. I pressed her hand down and goosed her boob, laughing that she was going to get us killed.

Fishing an instamatic camera from the glove box, she swung it around by its cord. "Look what I got in the casino gift shop," she said, "for our first pictures together!"

I slowed off the road and scampered to a waist-high sagebrush for quick relief. The volleyball player, who had been lost far behind, roared past with a bawdy blast of her horn. A bleating wind was the only sound that replaced the disappearing whine of her car. Liz was out, too, snapping pictures of the slanted orange canyons as I dodged thick branches of cacti getting back to the car. Far off, a dark bulb on the roadway moved toward us. The anxiety of being trailed had disappeared somewhat. California—the job, the cabin, the killings—was now a separate place.

Winding up gears to 75, I noticed the dark car in our rearview. From a small crate of catalogued tapes I plucked *Comes a Time* and held it to the dash as the motor pulled it in, and a tune half-sung broke through the speakers. Music of the desert drifter took me away, pleasant songs that settled on us like a wreath. Liz sat there looking contented, the tiny camera in her lap.

"That's nice music," she said. "I like it." I pointed to my shirt and smiled. The desert air blew through the car. Lime green sage nestled along the road, and I raced the road's dotted line, witnessing the Honda enlarge before us. We whooshed by as Liz snapped a picture. The blonde frowned at that, an insulted look in her eyes.

"What did you do that for?"

"There's nothing else out here," she said. "Maybe I'll keep a record of your old girlfriends."

I made a sour face. "Oh, come on." I eased into the right lane and put distance between us and the silver car. For a fair distance, I raced for Kingman, but as the road curved in a gradual bend, there she was again, passing. When I glanced over, she beamed and raced ahead for the right lane.

"Who is this girl?" Liz groused.

"I didn't want to say it, but here goes: That's my wife Robin in that car." I looked down. The dancing red needle was a tick above 70.

"Now I know you're lying," she grinned, "because you said you had a Mazda, and that's a Honda."

"Mm, you got me. Good memory. I have no idea who that woman is."

"Plus that woman seemed sober."

I laughed. "Boy, you are on a roll today." A highway sign appeared at the shoulder declaring the exit for Golden Valley. "Speaking of booze, let's stop up here and have a . . . you know what." I gestured tipping a bottle.

"It's warm out. I guess a glass of white wine would be okay."

Kingman's side streets coughed up cars into its thoroughfares, and the winsome highway was lost. At the exit ramp, we fell in behind a diesel-charred dump truck. The girl in the Honda honked a farewell beep, so I blew a kiss at the overpass. Liz socked me in the arm, called me a bastard while laughing, and we rolled along Old Route 66 until we slowed and stopped in front of an empty hamburger joint called Calico's.

In a roomy booth, I flipped open the atlas. Lipstick was being applied across the table and I set two separate fingers on towns. "What's our big hurry for Flagstaff? Can I ask that?"

The compact mirror was tipped and raised above her face as a line of faint rose glossed her lips. "What do you mean?"

"Well, this map here shows two ways of going, and I say take the Old 66 and leave the interstate alone."

She puckered her lips to a tight seal and edged a nail along them. The compact snapped shut. "Whatever you think."

An hour later, we were sailing eastward along the vintage path of her kinfolk. A sign marked CROOKTON lorded over a crossroads we rolled up to. Liz reminded me that we were not crooks, but the sign—was it an omen? I snickered and the transmission dropped to first gear.

As we neared Flagstaff, the spectacle began. Rising peaks were dusted with snow, painted reds and deep oranges at lower elevations.

I shivered with excitement. Liz snapped a picture through the windshield; the waitress at Calico's had already taken several for us. One of Liz mugging with her wine glass held high while I flashed a peace sign, Liz sitting on my lap a la the Buttonwillow tavern, even one of us in a newlywed's smooch.

Once in the Western town, we parked at an inn with a high reaching sign constructed in its namesake: HOTEL MONTE VISTA. Hoisting our bags and crockpot box, we jigged through the lobby and presented the clerk a small stack of twenties, and a second pile for the deposit. Liz shook her head, gripping the counter with a whispered refusal to occupy any suite with the word King in it. I remembered the comfort of my king-sized mattress back in Ohio. Instead, we were herded to a room with a queen-sized bed and private bathroom.

We chased down a room number in a dusty hallway. I wheezed as we walked. "I guess that whole 'no King room' will fade, right? I mean, it's kind of superstitious, isn't it?"

She sighed as I tried the key and the door jumped open, "Yeah, I guess so. Just a little too fresh right now. You have to admit, it's been a rough day."

I tossed my bag onto a chair. The box I secured inside a deep closet, pillowing a blanket around it. I clapped my hands. "You're right, it has been. This money of all things is a problem. Hauling it around, the chance of it being stolen. That cocktail lounge down there looked nice, billiards, too. But what, do we really want to go down to a bar with me carrying a crockpot box? They'll think I'm Billy Chili or something. Throw these people some crackers, that's what they'll say about us."

She smirked and spun down into a chair. "I guess I haven't thought about it all that much."

I fell back stiff across the bed, flung my arms open, and gazed at the stucco designs in the ceiling. "Who would ever guess that having cash money could be a problem?"

"Once we get settled in a place, though, you can just put it in the bank."

"I can't. It's not that easy," I said, propping a pillow beneath my head. Footsteps passed outside the door and a man whooped at two women's voices, one of them scratchy and foul-mouthed. She perked up. "Hey, I got an idea. I could go to a boutique around here—we saw that sign for Old Town shops—and buy a shoulder bag, one of those oversized purses. I could picture us at least having a drink in public without that stupid box."

Someone on the sidewalk below was singing loud and off key. I pictured the cowboy with his two ladies. "That'd work just right. Another thought? Same idea kind of, but you know those fanny pack bags I see dudes wearing? They look goofy as hell, but I could get one and put all the fifties in it. That way, if we got robbed, we'd have a better chance of getting away with part of it."

She coughed and moved over to the bed, dropping next to me. Her head rested against my shoulder. "Well, that's a real positive thought, Prince Charming," she said. She sat up, irked. "Robbed? Why would you say that?"

"Just being realistic," I said. I popped up and sat at the edge of the bed. "It just dawned on me. What we're doing is basically money-laundering. I learned about it in agent school. Now, $9,900 is the cap at the banks, that much I know, but I remember them telling us high deposits draw suspicion. So, we'll have to start lower, you know, in the six or seven thousand range. I guess we could open accounts at two or three banks, spread it out a little. But even then, it's twenty grand. We'll still be sitting on sixty thousand bucks." I sighed. "Shit."

I hadn't even noticed her rubbing my back as she sprawled behind me. "I got an idea—two," she said. "One, won't we be able to get rid of some of it when we rent a place?"

I shook my head. "That's not much. Even with a security deposit, that'll be, fifteen hundred, maybe two grand. What's your other idea?"

"I was thinking about the bank," she said and hoisted herself up.

"You want to rob it?" I laughed and wrestled her backward, her breasts mounding with a gentle shake. My free hand wandered over them and rested.

"You want to hear my idea or not?" she said, her chin dipped into her neck.

"Sure. We're at the bank. Then what?" I rolled next to her and watched my fingers tracing her clavicle line as she spoke.

"Well, couldn't we just ask them to, you know, exchange some of those big bundles of tens and twenties into hundreds without making a major case out of it?"

"That's possible. We just got to get anchored here without freaking out. You know, do just one thing at a time, do everything calmly, so we don't botch it like I did in Tehachapi."

"Well, here's one thing we can do right," she said and tugged me on top of her. For the first time, we undressed and had distracted sex, right to the point. I stopped moving in her and rose from the bed, heading for the bathroom. "What was that?" she yelled, as I ran water and dried off.

"I'm sorry," I offered, pulling up my pants. "It's just this other stuff hanging over us. I feel like I'm suspended in air. I just want to get things rolling so we can get settled."

Liz fussed with her hair and hung at the window, her head tipped at the street below. "You know something? I don't think we'll need to drive. Right across the street is a store that looks like it'll have those belt thingies, Mountain Sports. And when we came into town, I saw a place down the street that had cute clothes in the window. They'll probably have accessories. I could go there right now and get something, then come back and you go." I could hear the edge of her fingernail drag across the glass as I approached her from behind and hung my chin over her shoulder. An old couple tottered across the street at the crosswalk.

"Will that be us in fifty years?"

"Maybe," she whispered.

"Hmm. Yeah, you're right. You go first, I'll wait and unpack, maybe noodle with that TV." I reached for the remote. "Just one sec before you leave. I want to see if there's anything on about us."

"I sure hope not," she said, snapping a tube of lipstick closed with a careless toss into her purse as she pulled open the door.

The news I realized would not broadcast for two hours. Instead I fell hypnotized by *Mannix,* a rerun where a police officer had killed a man over a grudge but swore the killing wasn't planned. He was suspended from duty just the same.

"That's about right, too," I mumbled as the program cut to a commercial for Bartles & James coolers, "another cop on a wrongful suspension." Mannix had been assigned to investigate the killing, though I'd never heard of a P.I. investigating a municipal force.

A loud sound of footsteps in the hallway gave way to a clicking of the door handle, and Liz came bouncing into the room. Over her shoulder hung a tanned bag the size of an oversized couch cushion. She wheeled around swinging her hips from side to side. The bag evoked a tannery. "Wow. Nice purse," I said, smiling at the notion of Liz on a shopping trip.

Her cheeks glowed. "Do you love it? Because it wasn't free, but it's handcrafted leather by local artisans, and when I walked in there, it was the first bag to catch my eye. And I thought, 'he'll go for that one.'" Her voice sounded pleasant.

"How much was it?"

"With tax, one forty," she said with a wiggle.

I waved and nodded at the number. "Seems good, I guess. But it's nice looking, and you'll use it, right?"

"Of course, I will," she sang, "I love it." I hugged her and ran my fingers over the flap, working the snap. "And the best part is the color. It won't draw attention. After you left, I worried you might pick out something flashy. I know how you wear yellow."

She shuddered. "There was another one, purple floral print and a yellow starburst. It's funny you said yellow because that one did catch my eye."

I snatched up my wallet and reached for the door handle. "Well, so far, so good. I'll go get mine and we'll load them up. Then we can throw away that box." I hung at the open door and lowered my voice to a hum, "No cooking in the room, remember?"

"No cooking is right," she mocked. "You kind of proved that in bed," she said as I closed the door, shaking my head. I made the stairwell landing before the joke hit me. At the foot of the steps, I could hear her up there still, just laughing away.

Across the street I swung open the door to Mountain Sports and glided to an aisle with belt bags on hooks and unclipped their most expensive one. The black leather pouch seemed police-like hanging from my waist—a flashback to the old service belt with plated cuffs, a squeaky holster, and a radio. I browsed several aisles, kicking past kayaks and lanterns, shelves of water purifying kits. The store's stale air had a canvas smell to it. No music, no rambunctious customers. I could hear my own shoes squeaking.

On my way back up the hotel stairway, I gave way to suspicion and stopped short of our room. The hum of a woman's voice caused my heart to race. *Who was she was talking to?* With a quick turn of the handle, the door whooshed open. She hung on the phone, glanced up, but otherwise ignored my entrance. "Mm hmm, okay, I'll talk to you later." Similar words I'd heard from Robin when I'd caught her on the phone with an old beau. That itch of hers had lingered long after the wedding, and I found out she had enticed, not one, but two men to hang around for her little sneaky encounters.

Those had been antsy days. Robin had dismissed my accusations, swore the secret phone calls amounted to hocus-pocus. That is, till I saw her getting out of an MG convertible one night in front of our apartment. I was supposed to be off with the National Guard for the weekend and had returned a full day early. Pulling up to my house, I had jumped from the car and raced into the front yard as my wife's "friend" sped away into the black night.

Now, Liz sat before me, the warm phone back on its cradle.

"Who was that?"

"My dad," she said with a frown.

"Your dad. Really." I tossed the paper bag to the bed. Taking a chair and folding my arms, I rolled my eyes at her.

She looked puzzled. "Yeah, really. Why?" she asked, her eyes clear and bright.

I cleared my throat and tapped fingers at my elbow. "Just seems strange, that's all."

"Sheez," she said, "where's the trust? Remember, you're the one who lied to me, or do I need to bring that up again?"

"Okay, okay," I said, "what did you call him for, then?"

Liz stood up, her eyes flattened out. "I wanted to find out what the hell was going on over there. I think you'll be happy with what I just found out. And when I tell you, you might want to offer me an apology."

"I'm sorry, alright? It's a long story." Silence engulfed the room as our eyes went awry. "So, what'd you find out?"

She sighed, curled her lip into a smirk. "Well, here goes. You and I are in the Bakersfield news."

"What?"

"Yeah. You're right. They're calling it a double murder. My dad said they flashed pictures of the bodies on the TV this morning. He said he could see it was some kind of cabin."

Her voice refrigerated my senses. I felt nauseous and clammy. "Oh, my God. That's terrible. What else?"

She unfolded her arms and hands. "The only reason my dad found out so quick was because Brenda, Billy's wife, called Rex and asked him if he knew where I was. He said he had no clue, which was the truth. It's funny because it dawned on me just then that you've been right all along about not getting my family involved."

I leaned in and wanted to hug her to stabilize my own shaking hands. "Yeah, but tell me about this Brenda girl. Now she's the one who sold you out, right? The girl Stan was talking about, the one who gave you up for three lines of meth?"

Liz dropped her chin. "Yeah, that's her. And that junkie bitch thinks she'll just call my brother now and find out where I am? After setting us up to get killed, all for some meth. It's sickening, what she's become. She and I used to be best friends!" Liz compacted her lips then went on. "I warned my dad to tell Rex not to say anything to her, that she'd double cross me. As far as I'm concerned, that friendship died with Stanley. Friendship . . . pfft."

"Uh oh," I hummed, raising a finger, "whoa. It's settling on me now. The Red Hawks want blood, you got to know it. And this Billy guy, he's got to be the acting president now that Stan and Ronnie are out of the picture."

"Yeah, but you don't get it. Stan was the cook. I mean, *the* cook. They all told me that. And now, he's gone, Ronnie the killer's gone, the chemical money's gone, plus they got no crank because you guys confiscated everything but what he unloaded on the street." She looked delighted.

I stood there sorting through it. "What is it?"

"If you think about it, you took down the whole operation. That's ironic. All the Red Hawks have now are scraps. Those ATF guys should be giving you a plaque instead of chasing you down. Really, they should," Liz said with a clap.

Without realizing it, I was on my feet, pacing the room. "That's a nice thought, but trust me, I would rather not drive back to Fresno and ask for the key to the city, you know? And, now I'm wondering if you should have even called Bakersfield? I mean, I wonder if somebody's already asking for permission to trace your dad's phone line, you know? ATF, maybe? The whole thing's got me thinking if we've come far enough east to stay out of harm's way."

She raised her eyebrows. "Well, I wasn't on the phone long with him, and I didn't tell him where I was because of what you said before. I think we're good here in Flagstaff. I say let's just try and relax."

I breathed out and stood center room, my hands dug into my pockets. "I—I guess you're right."

Liz moved toward me and we embraced hard, my arm wrapped all the way around her. That same smell of her skin crawled inside me, back to a singular spirit. "I love you," her voice puffed next to my ear. "Now, tell me, why all the suspicion when you walked in?"

I drew back and plopped onto the bed. Liz stood there with forgiving hands at my shoulders. "I am sorry. I know it's not an excuse because you're not Robin, but when I was in the hall and heard you on the phone, I got suspicious. Back in Ohio I caught my wife talking on the phone with this one old boyfriend of hers a couple times. She kept blowing me off, calling me alarmist and a jealous asshole. Until I caught her one night getting out of his car. She was drunk. Her clothes were all messed up. Her pants even had grass stains on them. There was still sweat on her lip for God's sake. They'd just finished screwing, I know it."

"Oh, I'm sorry," Liz murmured, "What did she say when you confronted her?"

"That they'd been at a park, just to talk," I spat the lie, staring at the floor. "Eleven thirty at night, yeah, let's go to a sonofabitchin' park."

Her abdomen pressed against my neck, and Liz stroked my hair, raking her fingers in warm circles. She hummed against me. I felt warm again and looked up. I clasped her hand. "I shouldn't have second guessed you. I'm sorry, Liz."

"Forget it." She sat on the bed and chirped, "Now I want to see what's in that." Her painted nails reached for the Mountain Sports bag.

"Well, there's a little gift in there for you," I said, remembering the gag.

"For me?" she gushed with busy fingers. Was she imagining that I was presenting a diamond ring? *A diamond, now that's a thought.* Something subtle, not nutsy big, not even an engagement ring. And my money would buy it, hard-earned money.

She unraveled the fanny pack and held it up. "Nice," she said, studying the smallish box on the bed. "What is that?"

"It's a snakebite kit," I roared, throwing an arm around her and landing on the bed.

She shook her head at me. "You are so weird."

I poised a clawed hand above her and circled down to her belly and tickled her until she squealed. "It's in case we're out somewhere," I sighed, "up in a mountain cabin, and one of us gets bitten. I'd hate to die of a snakebite."

"Well, thanks. So romantic," she said. "What do you want to die from? Ever thought about it?"

"Yeah. Old age. In my sleep, you by my side."

She looked glassy-eyed at me, like the time I had made a remark about carrying her across a threshold after a nice wedding. "That's a nice thought."

"Hey," I announced with a clap of my hands, "we got some packing to do here, right? And I got these rubber bands from the desk to bundle the money." I drew out a gob of rubber bands from my jeans. The belt bag held four bundles of bills, one hundred in each. Once around my waist, the man purse felt queer. But twenty thousand bucks hung from my belt. And Liz's shoulder bag, though bulky, had room for seventy thousand dollars in small bills.

She sashayed around the room, flashing a smile, asking me if she looked natural. I laughed at her exaggerated toss of the head and said we needed to watch the six o'clock news before heading down to the bar.

"No getting drunk down there," she warned, "not in public, right?"

"I got news for you. Good news. I'm not much of a drinker. I don't even like the taste of beer to be honest with you, never did. Robin all but ruined that for me."

Liz stacked up pillows at the headboard and stretched out. I sat in the stuffed chair and locked in on the news channel at the top of the hour, wondering if they'd even report on California shootings here in Arizona. Ours was speculation as reports skipped through the broadcast, bouncing from national stories to pieces unique to Flagstaff—a summer festival, how to ensure your water's safe, the passing of a prolific war veteran. And just after sports, before commercial break, the screen flashed a dark image of two stretched out bodies wrapped in sheets, a paramedic kneeling by their sides. I sat bolt upright.

"Oh, man," I said, shaking my head. A bright red graphic behind the camera read METH MURDERS, in bullet-hole lettering. A blonde woman with crisp Nordic features tapped a thin sheaf of papers. She looked into the camera and rattled off the story.

. . . Thanks, Don, and let's hope for the best for Coach Bugel and the Cardinals' team on a fresh start this fall.

Well, sheriff's deputies in California's Inyo County responding to a call of shots fired came upon a grisly scene late last night. Before the clock struck midnight at one couple's mountain retreat, two Kern

County men lay dead from bullet wounds, and their killers? Nowhere to be found.

Authorities are saying that drugs were involved, that the two victims have known ties to California's methamphetamine trade. Pronounced dead at the scene were Ronnie Borrell, 37, of Bakersfield, and Stanley Gorman, 41, also of Bakersfield. Sheriff's deputies in Inyo County told Channel Two's own Tony Cooper that Gorman had been recently charged with possession of narcotics and felony possession of a firearm. That case was conducted jointly by the Kern County Narcotics Division as well as the Bureau of Alcohol, Tobacco & Firearms. As far as possible suspects, deputies told Cooper that the case is being turned over to the FBI in Las Vegas, although agents there could not be reached for comment. More on this story as it develops.

Up next, Scott has plenty on May's unusually cool temperatures we've been experiencing and how we might even see some rain over the weekend. Stay with us, we'll be right back. . . .

The screen went to a man hefting a bulging trash bag in his driveway as it exploded and trash spilled in all directions. An icon for Glad appeared. I turned off the television and gulped. Liz stared at the black screen, pressing her hands under her legs. She made a bursting sound with her lungs, "Uhh!"

"Nice, huh?"

"Yeah, all of a sudden, you and I are the criminals?" she howled, looking agitated. "They called us 'killers'?"

"That's it. And what's with the FBI? ATF's got a hand in that. I'm guessing this is their way of treating the case objectively. See, we did this one case where a rogue cop in a small department in California was stealing weapons from his department's weapons locker. Instead of that department doing its own investigation in-house, they brought us in. It was their way of appeasing the public. You let another outside agency with no political ties to the department handle it. It's just how it goes."

I tapped an index finger at my temple. "Hmm. So, reaching out to the Department of Justice makes sense in a way. ATF's calling up the big dogs to make a determination of what happened. That way ATF doesn't get caught issuing a free pass to one of its own, you follow me?" My voice, as I rambled through the explanation, grew more confident.

"Yeah, that makes sense, but we ran away," she whined. "They'll think we had something to hide."

"You're right there," I said, "but I know Brad, my boss. He's cool. And he's smart. And I'm sure the cabin scene's been secured by FBI agents in Vegas to process. They'll see what happened. The place just screams self-defense. Because it was!" I was shouting but Liz was nodding along. "And I can raise my hand under oath without worries—you can, too—that we didn't do anything but defend ourselves. That's it. That's our way out. I know, I know, it wasn't our home, but this isn't a case of breaking and entering. They tried to kill us, for God's sake. We returned fire because we had a right to, the right to bear arms. It's in the Constitution."

She waved at me to sit. "Take it easy, you're getting loud. You don't have to convince me. I was there, remember?"

"I know," I sputtered, "but . . . that news report was so damn one-dimensional."

She curled her cheek and pursed her doubtful lips. "I don't know, Gary. We're here, and they're back in Vegas. Those FBI guys are going to start looking for us. Plus, Brenda and Billy and the gang are already calling around. God, how I just want this thing to be over and for us to go away. I thought about what you said when we were at the Carrizo Park, how it would go, you know, run to the hills, stay at a cabin for a while and then leave the state and be free."

I unsnapped the money bag, slipped it from my belt, and moved to the bed, sitting next to Liz. I flung an arm across her knee. "Well, I didn't expect Stan to come after us with guns blazing. That was horrible. Lord, the feeling I had in that bathroom, staring those two down with that little single-shot. I'll tell you now, I didn't think we were going to make it out of that cabin alive."

"Yeah," she whispered. She leaned against me and traced the lines of my bandaged hand that was wrapped around her thigh.

My voice bounced around the room in a glassine narrative. "If I hadn't tricked those guys with the money, they would have had

us. I was scared then, more than I've ever been scared in my life."
I gestured with my free hand at the television. "And come on, this
ridiculous reporter telling it like she knows." More silence. "There's
no going back now, even if we wanted to. No, we gotta do what
we can do from this point on, do you agree?"

"Mm hmm. What about Mexico? Why don't we just go there?
I mean, this is America, and we're free to go. The dollar goes a
long way down there. Right now, we're not being charged with
anything, and we do have all this cash, and nothing's stopping us.
If we disappear for a couple years, what can they do? Red Hawks
won't follow us, the FBI can't follow us, so why not?" She was tapping my hand with her fingertips, and glossy hair tumbled to her
cheek. She looked good, her complexion radiant. Her lips, though,
tightened with worry.

"I don't know, it crossed my mind," I said, "but if we run to
Mexico, we'll look guiltier than ever. No, I say we set up here, play
it dumb, and follow through on our plans. If they come to us for
questions, we answer them, and go on our way. We have a right
to live here. I admit it, though, when you were talking just now, I
was thinking how Mexico sounded good. You know, the two of us
living somewhere along the Baja coast . . ."

"And?"

"And that's just no good. I don't want to leave my own country
thinking I could wind up on some FBI poster for God's sake. What,
a wanted man like Stanley? And then, what? Taken into custody in
some Mexican jail before they extradite us back here. Imagine how
we'd look on the news. Crossing the border is just more trouble.

"I say we get a house here, start calling it our own. If you
wanted, we could go first thing in the morning. I think it's best. If
we have to face justice, so be it."

"I suppose you're right," she said, "I mean, you got me out of
Stan's life. So, I do trust you. I do."

I stared at Liz, ran back several strands of hair from her eyes
and hugged her. "We'll be okay. I promise."

CHAPTER THREE

We walked outside of the hotel to Aspen street and stood under the marquee to the Monte Vista cocktail lounge. A saucy neon sign projected above the sidewalk, its namesake scripted in cursive and the whole thing lit up in festive yellow. Above the well-stocked bar, a second garish sign reminded drinkers where they were. The long hardwood barrier waited for us, lined with padded bar stools for guests of the inn. The place reeked of history with old photographs that blitzed the eyes of patrons. Liz and I sat down at the bar for drinks, weighted down with cash. It was a strange feeling, all that money. Darkness created by the dim lighting forced my eyes to adjust.

"Rum and coke, please," Liz asked of the blonde pouring cocktails.

"And can you pour me a Long Island Iced Tea?" I placed a hand on Leslie's back and studied the barmaid's eyes.

"Yeah, I've made those. They're really potent, you know that, right?" She gave an ornery smile.

I tipped my head toward the door. "Well, we only have to make it up to our rooms, so we should be okay tonight."

"Oh, guests of the hotel? Well, you save a dollar on each drink if you can show me a room key."

Liz jingled the key from her fingertips. "And when you're done, could you point us in the direction of a good real estate office here in town?"

"I can," she said with a flip of two empty cocktail glasses. "You two moving to Flag?"

"Maybe," I said.

"Well, I'll get those drinks for you," she said, fishing out bottles from the well. "Karen in the back, her mom's a good agent. A lot of people from town go to her. She's pretty fair from what I hear."

I flopped my arm across the bar. "Thanks a lot, by the way," I said. "We're new and could use somebody who knows the area."

"That's what people do here in town, help each other—well, most people," she said.

"Yeah, right on. I know what you mean," I said with a snort.

Liz looked at me with a puzzled smile in the overhead light. "Is everything okay?" Liz asked under her breath.

"More than okay," I said. "You look amazing tonight. The only woman I know that doesn't need candles or the moonlight."

"Phew," she snickered, "for a second there, I thought you were going to say something mean the way you were scoping me out."

The barmaid appeared. I turned toward her. "I'm Gary, by the way," I announced, "and this is my girlfriend Leslie."

Her cheeks flushed pink, Liz made a face. "Don't be weird."

"I'm not. You got no idea how long I've been waiting to say that to somebody. Honest." I stared into her eyes. I thought about our trials in the desert, how we had scripted dreams in coffee shops, and made love in the flowers.

The barmaid laid her hand across her heart. "That's so sweet. I'm Tracy, by the way." She made the drinks appear and we drank them straight through. Liz winked at me and asked for a second round. "I get what you're doing, by the way," she whispered toward me.

"You do? What am I doing?"

"You're revealing our identities so law enforcement will see we had an alibi later, aren't you?" She looked at me with her hopeful blue eyes. "You sly dog."

The drink swam through me all the way to my knees. "That's not it at all," I said. "This relationship has been one giant risk. And we both took it. I had a feeling of faith about you, I still do." I declared myself with a wave of my bandaged hand.

She grabbed my arm and gave me a peck on the cheek. "And I love you right back."

The second round showed up. Tracy seemed humored. "Let's make a toast with this round," I bellowed, glancing at a diminutive couple in the corner who seemed disinterested in our toast. I lifted the Long Island to my brow, glanced at Liz whose lips for the first time looked a little cockeyed. I laughed. She'd always been so matter-of-fact, so snap-of-the-lipstick efficient about everything. Because she had to be. "Tracy, you want to join us? I'll pay for your drink."

"We'll pay for your drink, Tracy," Liz corrected.

"Right, we'll pay for your drink."

For the first time since we'd set foot inside the place, Tracy seemed confused. She held up a finger and sauntered off from the bar. With a shifty glance into the kitchen, she returned on fleet feet, set up three shot glasses on the bar and poured in three shots from a motley bottle with a scripted Spanish name. "This is our best tequila," she explained, with a wry grin. "So, what's your toast again, Troy?"

"Troy?" I asked, irritated. "My name's Gary and this is—"

"Liz, yeah, I know. I got it. Make your toast already because I don't want to get fired for drinking on the clock." She tossed a white towel over the sink's faucet arm.

"Right. Well, here goes," I said, setting down the tea and lifting the shot, laughing at Liz's lips. I wanted to toast to her drunken lips. "To us getting here," I declared.

"That's it?" Tracy asked. "Getting here? You serious? How about to new friends? That's always a nice toast."

"Yeah," Liz jumped in, "I'll drink to that. To new friends."

"To new friends!" I stood up from the bar stool.

"And to old friends," the small older man called, raising an ice water from his booth. His wife turned her face away.

"Yeah, to old friends," I said, "even though I don't see any here at the moment."

The shots went down, one, two, and then Liz, three. I leaned in to her, the first Long Island doing a fair job of turning my strength to slush, the second one poured and prepared to pick up where the other had left off, and the shot, angry and new to my bloodstream. Liz slumped against me. The bulge in her bag, still draped at her shoulder, pressed into my oblique. I remembered the number, somewhere in the neighborhood of $67,000 in her purse.

From my pocket, I peeled out two twenty dollar bills and slapped them on the counter. "That's for everything," I told Tracy and studied the clock on the wall. No getting drunk when we're carrying the cash. And now? Liz looked drunk, Tracy had disappeared with a whistle, and I sat down, down, down. I slurped at the edge of the new cocktail.

"You feeling it?" I asked her.

"What, you from Mars?" Her were eyes heavy-lidded. "Of course, I'm feeling it."

"Should we finish these?" I asked, pointing at the new drinks floating before us.

"You said 'don't drink,'" she whispered.

I raised a lone finger. "Ah, I said, 'don't get drunk.'"

"So much for that," she laughed, throwing herself into my shoulder. I threw an arm around her. I leaned back and whispered against her neck, "You know something? The first time I put my arms around you at the bakery, it felt so strange to me . . . in a beautiful way."

When she heard that, she turned, puzzled. "Yeah?"

"And now it just feels right."

She sat back up, her face shining. "I understand."

"You want to know what makes this different?" I asked.

"No."

"It's the first time I think I ever got drunk with a woman," I slurred.

"What do you mean?"

"What do I mean? I'll tell you what I mean. First time I met Robin, we were just kids, and she drank four beers, one after another. But here's the thing. Every time Robin got drunk from that point on, she did it ahead of me. She was always trashed before I even got my first drink down. Like she was afraid that someone else might get tipsy first or have fun. So I had to sit around," I said, waving my hand at a conjured bar scene, "worrying about how much she was going to drink, what she was going to say to somebody, and then lift her up and carry her to the car, and then drive her home, and then she'd get—"

"I get it. I've been there myself, remember?"

"Yeah, I suppose," I said. "It's just nice. That's all I'm saying. Just nice. Drinks with somebody. Not watching somebody get drunk."

Tracy appeared from the backroom, sheepish looking. She approached and laid a realtor's business card on the counter. I looked at it, broken from the rush of booze, back to our dilemma.

"You two still doing good down here?" she asked with a wipe, the errant bottle resettled on its elevated shelf. She tugged at her hair.

"Yeah, we were just having kind of a moment," I said.

Before she could walk away, a small voice sounded off from the far side of the room. "Those two newlyweds over there could teach the rest of us a thing or two about love, Tracy," the small man said.

I turned toward him and threw up a hand. "Ah, just boyfriend-girlfriend here, that's all." Liz smiled at me. I turned back to Tracy, and leaned in with a whisper. "Who is this guy?"

"You know who that is?" she asked, her tone hushed with meaning. "That's Phil Wagner and his wife. He's the county commissioner."

Before I could come to a foggy comprehension of what a county commissioner does, we had pressed back our drinks, saluted the commissioner, and shaken hands with Tracy. Then Liz tugged at my sleeve and out we went, shuffling along a city walk and ambling into a sandwich joint not far from the hotel.

Our sloppy walk ended with us eating sizzling burgers on toasted buns, a great basket of fries spilling over the table between us. The monstrous cup of ice water sobered me up—somewhat. Somehow we managed to waltz back to the inn. We went weaving upstairs, tinkling with the lock. A guest down the hall shouted at us to go to bed, apparently for professing our love for one another. We clicked the key and rushed through the door, crashing to the bed laughing.

CHAPTER FOUR

That following morning, sunlight broke over a distant mountain range. I watched it light the sky while standing there in my underwear, scratching my armpit at the hotel window, waiting for Liz to stir. The door to the room hung open, a wedge of light across it. Shaking my head, I closed it and staggered into a chair. I dozed again before getting into fresh clothes.

I tiptoed down the stairs and pushed through the doors for some fresh air, wandering for several blocks. I returned for a pair of coffees, the early riser crowd having showered and spread themselves around the lobby, well into their local newspapers.

I was relieved to find that the shootings were not mentioned in the paper. I imagined seeing my face stretched across the front page and lambing it through the back door with my sleepy-eyed accomplice. Instead, I prepared coffees to a delicate whistle—one black, the other cream and sugar. I recalled how it had gone the last time we'd woken to hotel coffee. The revelation of my true identity and the argument that had ensued.

I went upstairs slowly. "Good morning," I said as she whirled around in a cone of blankets.

"Ah, this bed is hard," she said in a yawn, lifting a bent leg above the other and exposing her underwear. "It's not the casino bed, that's for sure."

"Well, well, well," I murmured, "good morning to you and your pink panties."

She snorted. "All it takes for you is a flash of underwear."

"You better believe it," I said, "You know, I didn't sleep well, either." I set down a cup and smacked my lips at the sludgy taste.

She sat up and palmed the coffee. "You know what dawned on me? We can't take jobs here in Flagstaff. Not yet, at least."

"What do you mean?"

She propped herself up on one elbow and lifted her chin at me. "When did you get up for coffee?" She braced it at the table and sat Indian style, pillows mounded behind her.

"I got up real early," I said, "even walked around the city block at sunrise. It's nice here. What a cool mountain town."

"Uh, I still got half a headache," she droned, tucking loose strands around her ear.

"Yeah, I guess we hit it pretty good last night, huh?"

She nodded and sipped.

"Bringing you coffee," I mused, "far cry from our time at the Marriott. Only this time I don't have any bad news. Speaking of news, we're not even in the local papers."

"Oh, that was a terrible morning."

"Yeah, so what's this about us not getting jobs?"

She jounced in bed and fluffed up the pillows, her eyes clear. "Do you think we should jump right into jobs, just two days after what happened?" I opened a hand to respond but she waved me off. "Hear me out. The guy on the news said that the FBI is handling this case, right?" I slurped the hot coffee and sensed the direction of her question.

"If we drive around Flagstaff putting job applications in everywhere and the applications ask for social security numbers and old addresses, can't the FBI run a check and find us that way?"

I shrugged. "Yeah, you're right. We've got to be the chief suspects in the case. They'll be looking for us to surface somewhere. I don't know how they'll trace us, though. Through the Social Security Administration, could they do it that way?"

Her fingers rolled the bottom of her night shirt into a cotton crepe and unrolled it while her eyes busied in thought. "None of this dawned on me till this morning. I was laying here while you were gone, thinking about how much fun it would be to find a new restaurant. I love waitressing, I do. But then it hit me. I'll have to put Village Inn down on the application. And as soon as they call back there to find out what kind of worker I was, I know what Chuck will say."

"Who's Chuck?"

She ducked her chin a little. "The guy with the flat top, dresses in the same polyester pants every day. I know him. He'd blab his ass off. All the waitresses say he's like a woman, pedaling gossip whenever he can. And my dad said the news of the killings is already all over Bakersfield."

I sat back in the chair and set the coffee aside, folding my arms. "Yeah, you've got something," I said. I stared at a room portrait of a solitary coyote. "What am I supposed to do for work? I can't go back to law enforcement, not now. Besides, I wouldn't want to even if I could. I'm sorry, I should have thought this out before we left the Valley."

"It's not your fault, you didn't know."

"Yeah, I suppose. I could go back to school," I said, "and get a degree in another field. I don't think colleges run a background check. All they want is your money. And I still have my old Ohio license, so I could get by." The loud cowboy and his woman came thumping through the hallway outside our door, whooping it up about a line in some movie. "Those people seem wild."

Liz stretched out to a prone position, stuffing a pillow beneath her cheek. "Yeah, they're pretty loud. But what about the immediate, huh? It sounds obvious, but what do we do today?"

"I don't know. How 'bout this? Nothing."

"Nothing?"

"Not a blessed thing."

She rolled to her back and burst out laughing. "You mean, just stay here in this hotel and wait for the FBI to show up?"

I waved my hand. "No, no, no," I said, grinning at a mental video of us, slumming it at the hotel, shuffling around the city, not a productive bone in our bodies. "I mean, let's go and rent a place right off, maybe month by month. I don't know what they got here, houses or apartments or what, but we'll need a place that's furnished."

"I want a house," she said, "that way no apartment neighbors can keep tabs on us."

"Yeah, me too. How 'bout a little cottage set off from the road, away from neighbors? I could do some landscaping and we could stay active at least." I ran fingers through my hair.

Liz nodded. "We should shower and go, maybe meet Karen's mom or even some other agent. I hope she's got a place where we can move in right away.

"And another thing. Once we pack up, I could call my dad one last time before we walk out, see what he knows. That way even if the call gets traced, we're gone before they get here."

I snorted and grinned. "You should be a cop yourself. You're right."

"Well, living with a druggie taught me some things," she said.

I laughed at her, wanted to jump on the bed and romp around. "I'm getting hungry," I said to no particular aim. A brick wall appeared. "Shit, I just thought of something."

"Having sex?" she giggled.

"No, but listen to you. Check it out, though. Remember what I said about the banks and depositing some of this money? I don't know why I just now thought of this—maybe it was the talk about social security. Either way, I'm almost positive you have to give them your social security number just to open a bank account. Which means we can't open an account. Which means we're still holding all this money. Which means lugging around two bags of cash. That's just great.

"We couldn't go to work if we wanted to, at least not at the same time during the day. We'd have to leave it at home. I'd be worried about someone breaking in and stealing it all. Damn.

"It's starting to settle on me now. No jobs. We can't bank the cash. We're living with the risk of a robbery. Sheesh. We're going to need to be cleared of all charges, everything that happened in the mountains, just to go on and live normal lives."

"I guess you're right, Gary," she said blankly.

"I'll be damned, though, if I'm turning myself in so they can throw me in some Vegas lockup while they get their shit together and bring us to trial. We know we're innocent, but, hey, maybe they won't even charge us, you know?"

She swung her feet to the floor and grabbed her open suitcase, flipping it to the bed as I watched her lay out fresh clothes, a stone-washed pair of jeans and a powder blue Cardigan sweater the same shade as her eyes. "Just a second. Why are you so sure we'll be charged?"

I rested my jaw on my fist as she peeled out of her pajama top, unsnapping her bra and rubbing her breasts without a care. "Because when someone gets shot, honey, no matter good or bad, they want the person who pulled the trigger to answer for it. Hell, even cops get charged in cases of self-defense. And that's even when they're . . . like totally innocent."

"Like totally," she mocked.

"You're a funny girl, huh? Maybe I'll come over there and hold you down and tickle you till you pee your pants." She stuck out her tongue and dropped her panties to the floor. "Seriously though, I am expecting us to get charged. But no way am I going up there to wait for them to charge us and arraign us. Let them come to us if they want us that bad. I feel restless, like we're pinned in an invisible corner."

"But for now?" She stood there naked as a jaybird. "I just want to know about today's plan."

"For now, let's go get some breakfast, pack up our stuff—okay, this is ridiculous, having a conversation with you while you're naked, you little joker."

"What?" she whined, batting her lashes.

"Seriously, then you can call your dad. After that, we'll flush out a realtor in this town and see if we can't find a place."

"Aren't you forgetting something?" she asked, a suggestive tone in her voice. She pushed me back to the chair, straddling its padded arms. Her fingers fumbled with my belt buckle, my zipper was down, and then I was staring Liz in the eye. Then she swayed her hips into my lap. But even while making love, my thoughts danced everywhere.

* * *

It was easy for me to see Karen Swayze as a mother who loved to cook, a doting grandma who spoils newly sprung grandchildren with ice cream cones and trips to the petting zoo. She was heavy with affectionate features and pronounced make-up. A trail of discriminating perfume followed her through the office. The place was plastered with property listings. Extending her hand, she jangled an enviable collection of thin, gold bracelets. I introduced Liz to her and those in the office. Karen impressed upon me that she wanted us to have "an absolutely great day," but what she said sounded more like a realtor's jingle á la Tony the Tiger. As we followed her to her office, I contemplated the slogan and glanced at a wall clock.

I supposed I was having a great day. After all, we'd eluded death in the High Desert, escaped to Vegas with over $85,000 cash, and arrived in this polestar among snow-capped mountains. Liz had just made wild love to me. Before we checked out, she'd spoken with her father by phone, and there were no developments to report from Bakersfield. While that was going on, I'd slipped off to the jeweler down the street and found a modest diamond in a plain mounting for $1,100. Liz had no idea. The box rode in my pocket while I waited to present it at a choice moment.

"You know what you just said out there?" I asked the agent, who looked surprised. "About a great day? Well, it has been for me. A damn great day, in fact."

"Well, that's . . . wonderful. I'm delighted to hear that," she said. "Now, Mister and Missus," she asked, her head moving about her desk, waiting for one of us to finish the title, a flourish of paper beneath her hands. One paper had the boxes one finds on an application, what looked like a litany of nosy questions running down the page.

"No, we're not married," I said, springing an empty chair forward for Liz, "at least not yet."

Liz tipped her head. "He's getting smarter every day."

I burst out laughing so loudly I startled Karen who fluttered through listings while we sat there. Flipping through homes of the Arizona landscape, I envisioned Liz and me, after the biker hassles and our entanglement with the law, working with our hands and making a simple life together. Some benevolent minister would introduce us as Mr. & Mrs. Whitehall and we could show up in offices like this one as a legitimate couple. Two young lovers peeling away for winter vacations in Mexico, wrestling with children of our own.

But for now, I had one eye on Karen's potpourri burner and the other on her stack of required documents. It struck me that everything you do in American life is tethered to paper. What kind of home were we looking for? And in what price range? More listing guides were slid across the desk, and we flipped through tiny photos of mountain homes, one picture in particular not unlike the Inyo County cabin. But Liz and I needed a place to sleep—tonight.

"Uh, Mrs. Swayze, is it? See, here's our situation. We're in town, and we're keen on it and all. But we need to get settled, find jobs, and then look for a house. Though, just out of curiosity, how much would this place in the middle of the page run us, assuming we could buy it?" I reached the guide across the desk, tapping my finger at a canyon ranch with sprawling eaves, the property bordered by a cedar post fence.

"Please, call me Karen. Alright, what's listed here is going for 216, so you'd have to write an offer first, and if they accepted it, who knows? Maybe you could get into that home for somewhere around 195, maybe 200. It's hard to say. That's guesstimating, you see." She wiggled and tapped her nails at her desk. Her thick brunette eyebrows furled in consternation. From the corner of my eye, I saw Liz smirk and then smile for Karen's benefit.

"How much on the down payment?" Liz asked.

"Depends, but 20% is preferred these days by most conventional lenders, so . . . you'd need to come up with forty to get things rolling," she said, a twinkle in her eyes. Her chubby fingers tapped continuously at the desk. I imagined with her commission checks, she could afford expensive perfume, the linen suit jacket, and those designer shoes, to say nothing of the luxury car I know she had parked outside.

I cleared my voice. "And how much would we pay monthly on a place like that?"

She whipped from her desk drawer a calculator, her nail tapping out digits, a smile intact while she worked. "This is an amortization calculator," she explained, "and the tax likely," she mumbled, "and the insurance likely," she mumbled again, "and with the commission and . . . you'd wind up around nine." She stopped working.

"Thousand?" Liz asked.

Karen's dimple creased into her cheek, and she made what I thought was a dismissive face. "No, honey," she said, "hundred. Nine hundred. Your payment would be in the nine hundreds somewhere."

"Ah," I said, relieved to hear. "I see that place is up in a remote canyon. Got any houses like that for rent?"

"Oh," she said and sighed. "You two are looking for a rental." The gay lilt in her voice disappeared. Whirling her chair toward a filing cabinet, she slung a drawer from its rightful place, fingered a few folders, and produced a stapled bundle. She slapped it on her desk and slumped into the exhausted chair. Listings ran down a column, some highlighted in yellow, others in black print. "I got two places for rent right now, both furnished, one here in town, the other outside Flagstaff a ways. Which sounds good?" She seemed impatient.

"I don't want to live in town," I said. Liz sat there, studying Karen with flattened-eyes. I remembered how Tracy at the cocktail lounge had characterized this woman: Fair.

"Well," she said, "that'll make it easy. We have this one home, at least one that will meet your current . . . needs."

"Yeah," I said, "I guess we'll go look at that one then, see if it 'meets our needs.'" I felt Liz run her soft fingertips across my forearm. "And maybe you should bring some papers with you, too. That way, if we like it, we'll just rent it on the spot, and you can write it up."

"That's going to require a security deposit on top of the first month's rent. You folks realize that?" she asked with a bluster of folders closing, a jingle of car keys.

"Yeah, Karen, we realize it," Liz said. "I think we can afford it, believe it or not." Liz turned her head toward me, and her blue eyes seemed gray.

"Oh, no, I wasn't saying that," Karen gushed, "I'm sure you folks are lovely people. I was just under the impression that you were—"

"Yeah, we know," I said and stood in front of her desk, Liz leading the way through the office.

"We're going to be going a ways out of town. Jerry, is it? This place is all the way north on Route 180 near the outskirts."

I gestured at the door for her to step before me. "That's perfect. And it's Gary, by the way."

The two cars turned through several intersections of Flagstaff and then we sailed along great sweeps of state highway. Before us, Karen's Mercedes Benz moved in a smooth line. "Tell me something." I waved at the car, its finish lackluster from the Arizona sun. "You get a whiff of attitude from this lady?"

Liz nodded and lowered her window. "Did I? As soon as you said 'rental,' she changed her tune just like that." She snapped her fingers.

"Yeah, I noticed. How about that?" I tapped the bulging fanny pack at my belt. "I should have pulled this out to change her tune."

Liz coughed up a laugh. "What, your wiener?"

I cracked up and the car veered into the road's shoulder before I corrected it. "You. Wow, that was a good one.

"Look, here's the thing. I'm too happy right now to get all uptight over some lady. Besides, look where she's leading us. This is nice country up here. And we did agreed that this is our day, remember?"

"Yeah, you're right."

Karen slowed and signaled for a mountain road and we ascended toward an orange-shaded ridge. Near its crest, she rumbled to a stop before a sprawling ranch. The place afforded a view of a deep butterscotch canyon. The agent was out and wheeling through the front door before we even had a chance to park. "Go ahead, folks," she said, shooing us through the door. "Take a look around. The owners have left on the utilities and said the tenant will need to call the companies on the paper here on the kitchen counter." I turned from the picture window to see. "That's just to transfer them into your name. But for now, you've got water, electric and electric heater, and the phone. Plus there's the big fireplace when it gets cold, and I'm sure you saw the stacked firewood coming in." I nodded that I had. "Though it's furnished, take a look around. Off the record, I'd say the place needs a good overall cleaning. But the two of you seem full of energy," she said, "so maybe it's a good fit."

"Yeah, that and someone long on love for hiking the canyons," I said. Liz looked at me. "What do you think, Liz? Is it a keeper?"

She grinned and came across the room. When she hugged me, there was that same vanilla smell. We toured the place and agreed to rent it on a monthly basis—which we all agreed was a blessing. I produced $1900 cash, all in $100s. The papers were signed and with a wave, Karen was gone. It was quiet then. We looked at one another. Then I hooted and Liz jumped into my arms.

Outside we opened the Honda's trunk and set off for the front door with the first of our bags. I stopped on the front porch and asked if she wouldn't mind setting them down. She stooped to the wooden decking, her nose squinting. I stepped between her and the luggage. Slinging my arm around her, I hoisted Liz across the threshold. "I wanted to do this," I said with a grunt. "You know that."

"Oh, that's so nice," she said with a bump. "You made good on the promise."

I whispered, "That's not all." I drew the boxed ring from my pocket. "Some people I know would say this is premature, but I don't care. We've been through a lot fast. I feel like I've been look-ing for a woman like you my whole life. That's why I walked away from everything. I want to start over and make things right."

"*Gary,*" she said in a strange pitch.

Her eyes wetted and she pawed them. "I know, I think the same thing. I went home after we met at the bakery, and I think I slept an hour that night." She laughed through her tears, which seemed strange to me. I'd seen women bawl at weddings, weep over a sad movie, but had never understood it completely.

I flashed back to Robin, who had only grinned when I proposed—no tears, no choked confessions of love. Instead, she had made a wisecrack about me being corny. I flushed that scene from my mind.

"That second time you came to the Village Inn, my heart was beating so hard. I couldn't keep my orders straight! You could probably tell," she said. I shook my head and touched her wet fingers. "Can I open it?"

I nodded. "But I should first explain something. Until I get matters settled with Robin back in Ohio, we'll just have to go along as boyfriend-girlfriend. Is that okay with you?"

"Of course, I'm happy to be your girlfriend. And to tell you the truth, Stan never bought me a ring. He never bought me anything, for that matter," she choked.

"Not anything?"

She shook her head and sat back on the couch, the box poised in her fingertips. She opened it. "It's beautiful," she whispered. She slid it onto her spread finger.

"The lady at the store asked me to guess your ring size by getting me to hold her hand. Her fingers were average size, that's yours. It's a six, by the way," I said.

"It's so nice," she whispered. "It's perfect for me."

* * *

By the following day's sunset, we had unpacked everything, set up an insurance policy on the car via telephone, and had cleaned the entire ranch from wall to wall. Then we hit a Safeway for groceries. That first night, I smoked salmon on the grill while she tossed a salad and warmed bread in the oven. On the back deck, we sat back in Adirondack chairs while the sun spread reds and oranges across the summer sky. The dry canyon air cooled like a falling blanket once the sun left us.

"A road trip," I announced, sitting there with a bottle of beer in my hand. "We should take a road trip together. Just go and tour the whole region. We got no reason not to."

"That sounds fun," she said. "What, just take the money with us?"

I shook my head. "Uh-uh. That's bad news if we get robbed. No, this morning when we were cleaning the place, I found nine or ten cubbyholes that would be perfect for stashing money. I was thinking that'd be smart, bundle it up in groups of ten thousand and separate it. There's places in the garage—I'll show you where—I know no one would look if we hid it there. Plus inside, there are sliding compartments. I can tape and fit some of it under that back sink. When we leave, we just lock it all up. This place is a fortress from what I can tell. Did you check out their deadbolts and the security system? It's wired into the county dispatcher's office.

"That way, even if the worst happens, the cops raid us, they won't find it all. Before we leave, we'll hide eight bundles and take—what, five thousand with us? And we can always get travelers' checks at the bank for that."

"Why not?" she cried. Then we went to bed in a drowse and climbed beneath freshly washed sheets, all cool and fluttering down.

CHAPTER FIVE

Long before we made West Texas, my girlfriend and I had split Coconino National Forest on bone dry bi-ways and stone passes. On Liz's dare I started off for New Mexico. We found ourselves dazzled by native lands rich with burnt oranges and mud-rich cocoas, passing stratified cliffs. At an isolated adobe house, a wavy-haired Spanish woman stopped hanging clothes and waved. Her place backed into a canyon, a narrow finger shading the home.

A sign in the shape of a kidney appeared on the horizon, and we pulled in front of a squat building all scuffed up. The dingy front door of El Nuevo Sonido was open and we walked into the lonely bar. Off in a corner purpled by a bar light, several musicians tinkered with instruments. Somewhere in the back corn tortillas were baking and the rich smell filled the room. We sat down and waited, tapping hands and sipping Cervezas.

A guy who called himself Acoustic Bill stepped up to the mic and nodded at us as he sat down and whistled on steel strings. Some Mexican guy played folk music on harmonica, and they had a third player on piano. When a veteran wearing an eye patch started plucking banjo strings, Liz was tapping her feet so I asked her to dance. She bounced around the empty room until we were both sweating and thirsty for more beer.

Just outside, in a Silver City gift shop, I bought Liz a pair of stylish, cat-eyed glasses. We kissed outside the place, a cloud of blue swirling back into my eyes from the reflection of her sunglasses. Then I spread the map across the hot roof and followed my finger through the New Mexico roadway into Texas, where we stayed the first night.

With coffee on the sunrise dash leaving El Paso, I listened to the little sounds of desert crosswinds, pulled in and pummeled by the car's rushing locomotion. There was a joint called Key the Sky in the middle of nowhere, so we stopped for Texas chili and chatted with a waitress who had the personality of a junkyard dog. Later in the car, Liz said she was snarly and suspicious. On the big dry side of Odessa, where the Union Pacific barges through Pecos, just north of the 20, we checked into a clean motel with a bright red roof. It sat next to a zoo the size of a schoolyard.

She laughed when I mumbled that I was hungry enough to eat a sheep. So we shot along the rail line to a little free-standing adobe shack with a hand-painted sign out front. We sat on white plastic chairs on the back patio, eating Mexican food from paper bags. Slowly the cool of the desert crept around us. And I marveled at clouds reaching such incredible heights. Loose orange eels stretched toward the sun, which raced from the encroaching dusk. The Union Pacific roared by and echoed for miles away and then silence.

Then the birds started.

How queer it was to see a tree filled with rare birds—flickers, woodpeckers, warblers—reds and flaming oranges and songs and shrieks I'd never heard in Ohio. For us it had always been some caged finch sealed in by a frosty winter. And the balmy winds of Texas moved past slowly. We sat there eating tostadas with enormous olives, sipping Mexican broth, waiting for the dope sick sun to set, and listening to jungle birds squawk. I felt like a sailor who has taken in a thousand ports around the world. It dawned on me. We were free.

Night fell and I shivered and the birds stopped singing.

* * *

Three days later we were back home. We began taking long hikes and found a great trail to a very lonely cliff. Kissing at the crest of a five hundred-foot cliff was a rush. Its cut face, a sheer drop and certain death, left me giddy. Liz waved her arms at the expanse and claimed high rights to Grand Canyon winds like she'd done with the California stars. I laughed and told her that she needed to stop taking meth, and she pushed me, and we wrestled until our lips met again.

In the distance, a pale horse appeared, its rider steering toward our home. I felt more curious than alarmed and we began backtracking for home. We arrived earlier than he and I made a stiff drink in my coffee mug and wandered out back. The rider approached, and the scene reminded me of an old Western movie. The horse's eyes were deep set and dark, like its gray-frocked rider's. The guy looked to be a drifter, slouched over in dusty breeches, a pair of horn bags behind him. I glanced at the horse's hind quarters for a rifle. Nothing. I paused at the patio, set down my whiskey sour, and got the sense I was looking at death.

"How you doing?"

"Not bad." He nodded like some Hollywood actor with grey almonds beneath his eyes. I almost expected a holster on his hip with a long-barreled Colt slung deep in it. There was none.

"Can I help you?"

"I was wondering if I could trouble you for a drink of water," he said. The guy seemed lost. Liz must have been eavesdropping because I heard water running at the sink and the clatter of glassed ice cubes. She was at my side then and reached it across the fence.

He took a long agitated drink, his throat lean and bony. "You know the way to town?" His voice was wet.

"It's that way," I said, lifting a half-drunk arm toward Flagstaff. I was on the deep end of my drink, ice cubes ballooning around in there. After the rider trotted off, Liz pattered back into the house, wondering aloud who that was. I shrugged and turned back to canyon gazing.

Within an hour I had passed out on the couch in the living room. I woke up to Liz tugging at the collar of my shirt. "Gary? Gary. Wake up."

"Yeah, what is it?"

"I've been thinking. We still got plenty of spending money. Let's go," she said, "and let's just keep going."

"Why do you want to leave all of a sudden?"

Silver earrings accented her hair and vanilla skin. But her eyes looked empty. "Because, that's why. Do I have to have a reason?"

"Well, I don't know if you do or you don't. I just asked."

"Alright. Because people don't take the road they've never been on. It makes 'em feel safe. And that's how I've lived up till now, in a little box in Bakersfield. That's why. How's that?"

I sat up smacking my lips and reached for the coffee mug with the whiskey in it. I toasted her with groggy eyes as she smoothed her fingers along my jaw. I felt her without using my hands, understood her without thinking.

At daybreak, we got into the car and off we went again, into canyons of colored stone cut by jets of water. We could see where glacier stone had become a burden to the short-sighted miners out for a quick nineteenth-century buck. I was still reeling, my tongue boozy from the night before. We started drinking from an oversized bottle of vodka, splashing citrus in cups, and we kept at it . . . all down the road.

Weaving through immense valleys and hard pressed passages, we speculated on strangers who ran the sluice and penstock for the tin-panners, splitting rocks, mighty rocks. Rocks symbolic of men who stood still in streams, hosing and breaking them through sheer vibration. For the third time my cup was empty.

Just past a dry gulch, a little town squatted in the sun before us. Little puffs of smoke signaled life. Liz pointed and insisted we go. A black locomotive clambered at their old fashioned train depot, where a stern-faced conductor unfolded his pocket watch. We rolled slowly past as a handful of travelers boarded. The ice machine inside the depot was on the fritz, and a Mexican woman using broken English pointed at a gas station down the street. They'd never had ice, I soon found out. From the station we roared down a desert road, a high-cloud rooster tail behind us. Before us a lone butte stopped the car. The rock was four stories high if it was one, not a soul in sight for miles of otherwise unbroken desert plain.

We walked around, kicked the orange dust from our shoes, and climbed back in. Liz filled our plastic cups again with vodka and a cheerful serving of cranberry. She waved her hand toward a tumble down boulder.

"You know, how you said back there all that stuff about faith in love?"

"Uh huh."

"Okay, that boulder there. Does it have faith, too? You know, what you said about the will to believe?" Her face slackened and bleached out in the bright sun.

"You're drunk," I laughed, easing back onto the long highway.

"I'm not either," she giggled. "If that big stone back there yields a quarter pound of gold, does it have faith? And if it had none, would the gold disappear from it? See, that's my question. It's not that hard to answer." Her head orbited on her neck, resting back on the seat, a pleasant numbness on her face. I wondered if she was going to pass out. I winced at the memory of Robin embracing a toilet, retching in great heaves, her bare ribs exposed and jerking beneath the skin. And me always with the pine cleaner and mop.

"Maybe we're drinking too much, huh?" I steadied the cup in my hand. "And I got to admit, this drink isn't good warm. We need ice. Next store we see we'll stop. Hey, and maybe we'll run into a Red Hawk biker." I thought of the Chevron up in Tehachapi.

"Ice?" she asked. "What about faith in Flagstaff's snow?" She was slurring her words. "Or, how about that high wheat we saw bundled? The stuff clinging on the bed of that train?"

"I don't know," I said, clearing my throat and pushing back memories. I felt a little ill myself, imbued with the spirit of the West and the spirit of the half-empty bottle now rolling around the rear floorboard. I saw myself a hundred years before, out from Ohio, spurred on for the Golden State in 1890. And in the eyes of the people, I would have been a pale, scrawny Easterner, one with linen handkerchiefs and bad lungs who had left Ohio's corn fields. A white man who never understood the medicine man's sun and spiritual winds that settle into the upper reaches of the desert.

"Hey!"

"Huh?"

"You okay?"

"Yeah," I said, "I'm fine." I finished my drink and she slopped us both another. The West glowered at me, and I caught myself wandering into a raised cloud of dust off the road before righting us again.

"What are you thinking of over there?"

"You really want to know?"

"Yeah."

"I spilled blood in Bishop, that's what. I made claims on another man's woman. I wonder if I'm damned."

"What are you talking about? I thought we agreed to forget that shit?" Her eyelids flickered.

"What am I talking about? High winds, that's what. Powder blue sky. Blinding snow. It's true, what we've done. I pulled a trigger forged with money. It was easy to do. Satan followed me to those mountains." The voice coming up from my chest dragged.

"You're not making any sense right now. It's a bunch of blather," she slurred. "Hey, Gary!"

"Stop yelling. I do feel weird right now, like something's lifting me out of this car, a spirit. Sierra Nevada graves, you know? They're untended, each man sold out, a woman raped under a constellation, all for an abstraction, say love or bravery."

"What the hell? Hey! You got to stop this. It's scaring me."

The tires felt fat at the end of the steering wheel. "And readiness became the consonance, Liz—the countenance, excuse me—of the beaten down. The fire of Stanley flickered and died." My brain seemed muddy, my head hot in all this. I kept driving into the big empty. I drove with my hands gripped hard there, then Liz was out cold on my shoulder. And the old man back in the Fresno office, I was sure, had sighed and measured the fire that had dwindled. We needed to stop. Rest for the day and night, get some food and stop all this blurry nonsense.

I parked at a mammoth adobe place marked INN. I set my feet down in the parking lot. I hoisted myself up and demanded that my legs walk in there to the desk. *In there.* Through those glass doors. A pair of eyes was looking out, a man's eyes. Black-framed glasses. I looked back at the car. *Shit.* Car door was still open, the buzzer sounding, like a locust on a tree. Thing was, do I go on in or go all the way back over there? Liz, she was slumped against the door like human mush. I was standing still but wavering here.

A fellow in a white collared shirt was at my side then passed me. He was at the car door and slammed it. Loud.

"Hey, what are you doing there?" I asked him, my mouth like Arkansas cotton. A little stringy feeling.

"Sir, are you okay?" he echoed, saying it twice. He brought those black plastic frames near my nose, studying me over. He smelled like oakmoss.

"Yeah, I'm fine," I said. "We just need to sleep." I burped up the words, my lips tight again.

"Well, come on in, sir," he said, and he steadied me at the elbow. I looked down. "What the hell you doing?"

"Let's get you some accommodations, sir, before one of the deputies comes by. How would that be?" he asked, swinging the door open. We went reeling across there, then he left me standing at the desk, holding on.

"Yeah, we been drinking," I confessed, my head still swimming. "But I got money for a room, and if you can help me and my woman out there—she's out cold. If you can help us get into a room, I'll tip you . . . good."

He went to tabulating a bunch of stuff back there, snapping off words and I just got tired and set my head down, just for a minute to rest.

"Sir, sir!" he shouted at me.

"No need to yell, man," I said. "Whatever I owe you, take it out of this," I blurted out and slapped my bundle on the desk. I saw him peeling off the money, but I studied his eyes. Honest eyes. Nervous looking but eyes true to purpose.

"You're a good man, I can tell," I said.

Next thing I know, he was lugging our goods up to the elevator. And pulling back the blankets for a big fat sheet all the way across there. I crashed across starched cotton and breathed into it.

"Sir, no sir, we can't sleep just yet. Your wife's still out in the car."

"Oh, yep," I chipped in with him and hoisted myself up like a dummy on a string. "Yep, yep. I'm coming. Let's go get her." I was holding on to the elevator thing, the rail thing in there. My stomach was sloshing back and forth, soup in a big kettle.

"What's your wife's name, sir?"

We came out, looking at the parking lot. It was so bright out there, the dirt blinded me. "My wife? Her name's Robin. Hey, we still got to walk all the way out there?"

"Yes, sir," he said, his arm tied around me somehow.

"Did you take a tip from my money?" I wondered.

He was at the other side, pulling her up from slumping over, up to her feet. She was licking her lips a lot, thirsty too. "No, sir, we're not permitted to take tips. Ma'am, can you stand on your own? That's good. We're just going in here and get you folks some rest, okay?"

It reminded me. I wanted to know something. "Where's my money, Hank?"

"Sir, remember, we went over this already. You put your money, all of it, back in your pocket. And my name's Jerrod, sir." Robin was next to me, holding me up or me grabbing her. Her shirt smell was close to me.

I leaned into her ear on the elevator. "We need to tip 'em," I said. I saw her nodding at me, smiling goofy that way. At the door, Hank looked tired, a little sweat on his lip there.

"Now, Robin, I can get the door open if you can hold up your husband—"

"Robin?" she hollered. "What the hell?"

"Okay, folks," he said with a whoosh of the door and we raced in there and my face was in soft white again and I breathed and wrestled with the cushion there, and then it was all black.

* * *

It was black when I awoke, quarter of five, my yellow head spinning among satellites of pain. Among the room's silhouettes, I made out luggage and dragged a familiar piece to the bathroom, closing the door. I stripped and got into the shower, washing my hair and ever so slowly reclaiming my equilibrium. I dried with brisk flaps of the towel and popped the door, dressing gingerly and studying Liz, open-mouthed across the bed. On the floor stretching from my pants pocket sprawled a fat wad of cash. I counted it again, same what I had yesterday—down forty some dollars. I held up to the bathroom light a folded receipt reporting the same amount. That Freddie or Hank or whatever his name was. Here it was on the bill—Jerrod.

That guy deserved a tip, I thought, and once I had my shoes on, I went down to the front desk and made that my first order of business. A young Mexican woman with her hair in a bow, pulled back so tightly it shone, met me at the desk. She provided me with a hotel envelope and an ink pen, in which I slipped a $20 bill and on which I wrote a heartfelt note of thanks, addressed to Jarrod.

Hot coffee waited in urns by the lobby doors. With a steaming cup, I pushed past the doors and made my way across the parking lot to the Prelude, sipping as I went. Its windows still down, the Honda had been parked cockeyed, and a neighboring driver had taken offense at what he must have surmised as a superior attitude or blatant carelessness. The Lincoln with Texas plates was parked no fewer than half a foot from my driver's door. Any other time, I would have thought, *asshole,* but this one was mine. I leaned in from the passenger side, removing the lukewarm spirits, the car's interior still damp from nightfall. It smelled sugary sour from abandoned cups of booze.

Otherwise, nothing had been disturbed, no pranks played, no rainstorm had come to Grants, New Mexico, during the night. I dumped the cups, went for two bottles still in the trunk, and threw them into a large Dumpster out back. Glass shattered the quiet, and I saw in the eastern distance the first shades of morning skies. Crawling back into the car, across the bucket seats and into the driver's side, I started the car, even considered writing a note of apology to the big Texan. But I was hungry.

At a 76 station down the street, I refilled the tank and feasted on a breakfast burrito before returning to the opposite side of the hotel. Then I took off on foot toward the distant mountain range, just to stretch myself out, to breathe from the earth and to forget what had happened. One or two far off cars motored along the big highway as I trekked around a big cactus and studied up close a saguaro bush. The morning air was heavy with sage.

When I returned Liz was sitting up, flicking sleep from the corner of her eye. She yawned and groaned, "Oh, I feel terrible," and then she fell back into bed.

"Drink this, you'll feel better," I whispered, remembering how sound-sensitive I'd been upon waking. "I made it like you like, cream and just a little sugar."

"Thanks," she said, sitting up on an elbow. "How are you?"

"Pfft, lousy. What a stupid thing we did yesterday. We could be in jail right now. That guy—you remember the guy that met us in the parking lot?" She sipped and squinted yes with her eyes. "Well, that dude deserves a hero's celebration. He got us in here safe, but the car, whew! I was just out there. Thing was sitting there taking up two spaces, windows still down, drinks just left there in the open."

Liz scratched at her shoulder and furrowed her brow. "You're kidding."

"No, I'm not. Nothing was taken, all my tapes and our stuff in the back, but it could have been. I threw out all the booze," I said.

"Good move there because I haven't been that drunk since I was in high school. What were we thinking?" Her eyes darted around the room that was growing lighter in shades. "Oh, I need a shower in the worst way, and some breakfast."

"Yeah," I waved at her, "I am not drinking again for a very long time."

She swung her legs from the bed, nipped at the coffee, and began shaking her head. "Let me tell you about this dream before I forget it in the shower. I had an awful dream about that other hotel back home, the Courtyard. Probably because you said something about it yesterday. Only you weren't in this dream.

"It was Brenda. Oh, my gosh. Brenda had this methamphetamine face. She was standing in the corridor on the third floor right by the elevator. All of it made me feel so weird that I woke up wondering if Brenda needs me or something, you know, a premonition. Now I just feel terrible."

I patted her back. "Well, it's over now. Get a shower, and you'll feel better."

CHAPTER SIX

The thin air of Albuquerque to the east bore elevated balloons in the distance. Collectively, they looked like a crayon box of colors floating over buttes and mountains. As we neared the city and stopped to gas up in a filling station, the balloons' burner jets burst on and off above us in brilliant yellow flames. The popping noises and tiny hands of those standing in the basket looked touchable just two hundred feet up.

A greasy-haired attendant craned his neck. He mumbled that the celebration of hot-air balloons was "nothing but a trial run" for the great festival to be held in the fall. We trickled into town, were parked by late afternoon, and canvassed the crepe paper streets brought to life with glittery streamers and barkers. We witnessed a chainsaw carving competition for over half an hour.

"You folks stick around," one vendor called, "fireworks display is all set for tonight." Liz hugged a stuffed panther and an oversized box of caramel corn. We munched handfuls during the street clown's juggling, long wooden pins flipping hand to hand. Moving people passed us, most faces happy in the setting sun. Then the neon lights of the street emboldened storefronts and merchant stands.

One lady was busy bending lime glass, twirling tubes into distorted lengths and decorative frames. I made the mistake of taking Liz's insistent hand aboard an oblong motorized car that began spinning while rotating as well. Some fifty feet in the air, above the street's rising heat, a disc jockey's voice garbled over the nauseating thump music, a screechy sonic dance. The Mexican pizza I'd had with a Coke came close to bubbling up. That was just before we were set down at the exit plate of the sputtering engine.

Just before we left to find a place to sleep for the night, Liz dropped a handful of quarters into a pay phone and called Bakersfield. I looked through the window of a general store and leather shop—until she showed up next to me. In the reflection of the store's glass I saw her arms cross. Then I heard her sniffle. When I turned, her face was puffed red, aflame with tears.

"What's wrong?" I asked, and an Hispanic woman clutching a child at each hand moved them away from our conversation.

"It's Rex," she bawled, pressing into my shirt and clasping an arm around me.

"What about him?"

"Oh, Gary," she cried.

"What? Tell me."

"My dad said Rex went by the cycle shop he always goes to in town, and a bunch of gang members jumped him coming out. It was Billy," she cried, "he was the one. That chickenshit. You know what he did? He had those other bastards hold my brother down behind the place while he threatened to hit Rex in the face with a bike chain. Unless he told him where we were."

"What? You kidding me, he did that?"

"Yeah."

I looked at her wide-eyed and moved her away from the street and several inquisitive faces, into an open-air corridor flanked with empty benches. "So," I began, helping her to a seat, "did he?"

"Tell him?" she said and shook her head. "No. He doesn't know where we're at. I mean, he swore to them 'Flagstaff's all I know—'"

"Aw, shit! He said 'Flagstaff,'" I swore. I grasped my face and rocked forward. "Shit, shit, shit."

"Just listen to the rest," she said. "So, my brother told him what he knew and swore that was all, so Billy hit him with the chain anyway."

"In the face?"

She nodded and huffed, "His face is all messed up, it puffed out his mouth in the shape of a plum, my dad said. Cut open his lip on one side so he needed stitches. Plus, Billy hit him hard enough to chip one of his front teeth."

I sat there, shocked, my hands perspiring at my knees, Liz sobbing and her nose running. I trotted off for a tissue, some air to think. "I'll be right back," I called. In seconds, I continued. "So, where's your brother now?"

"Dentist," she said, wiping the tears away and blowing her nose.

I dropped my elbows to my knees, looking away. Red Hawks Motorcycle Gang. *It's the money. They want the money.*

"My dad . . ." she said and paused. "My dad goes, 'you kids need to turn yourselves in and claim self-defense before anybody else gets hurt.'"

I sighed and folded my arms, just staring. Brilliant red azaleas skirted the corridor. "I'm sorry, honey. I'm sorry they went after your brother all on account of me. I'm sorry you had to hear about it like this, so far away. I know I'd want to be there with my family."

She gave a pouty smile, her lip stuck out a little. "It's okay."

I stood up over her at the bench. "No, it's not. I think we should go now. Go back to Flagstaff, that's a five-hour drive. We can't stay here in Albuquerque, not with this hanging over us." I threw out a hand and she took it. I hugged Liz hard, her shoulders melting into mine.

Once we were buckled in, red lights kept me from speeding out of town. With tires squealing, I dodged a trash can in the street. We sped through Old Town and shot onto Interstate 40, and it wasn't until I could see the town disappearing in our review mirror that I began to relax. The car's vents sucked in sweet desert air that blanketed the night, and Liz rode along in silence.

The highway felt endless, our headlights bleeding into oblivion until we hit the outskirts of Flagstaff. I pulled into a no-name gas station run by some guy named Hector peddling low octane fuel. I made the mistake of asking about the gas that I'd pumped. It was on account of the elevation, he said, thinner air creating a different fuel mix than what we have back East. While he went on about refineries and motor performance in broken English, I stood at the door, waiting for him to stop for air so I could duck out. I noticed a psychedelic poster on the door promoting an upcoming biker rally at a nearby lake. I pointed and asked, "This Forever Resorts, they're hosting some bikers up there?"

"Si, senor," he said, shaking his head. "That lake is no good. Very shallow, it's dry. They say they want place for all bikers to come every year. But the people here say no, they don't want the strangers. It could be trouble, you know."

"Huh. So, this is the first time for it?"

"Si."

I thanked him and then made an exit for the car. "Well, that was interesting," I sniffed, dropping the emergency brake handle and starting the car.

"Yeah, what was that all about?"

"Two nights from now, there's going to be a biker rally south of here. It's down Route 3 at a place called Mormon Lake. You pick it up off Interstate 17. That's the road to Phoenix."

Liz made a face as I turned onto the road home. "So, it's a biker rally. What about it?"

"I'm thinking about going down there," I said, clearing my throat.

"What?" she screeched. "Why? Why go down there? It'll just cause trouble."

We came to a red light. Downtown Flagstaff had fallen asleep, save for a pair of late night carousers and a police cruiser sitting in a parking lot with fog lights glowing. "No, I'm just wanting to see if, you know, any Red Hawks are going there."

"You're going to go to a biker rally, unarmed?" She said each word slowly, as if she were getting it straight in her own mind.

I nodded. "Yeah. The problem is I can't buy a handgun now, unless I get it off the street. They'll trace us here for sure if I get one at a dealer."

"Well, I don't like it," she said, her voice ragged. "Go down there and you might get hurt."

"I just want to cruise by, you know, maybe pick up some binoculars at that Mountain store. Just to see if we're being followed. That's all. Answer me this: Do we even want to stick around this town if the Red Hawks are tracking us?" A mood of panic, from being traced to the cabin, reminded me of my fatal nap and ill-timed hike to the mountain top.

The rental house we found empty. We dragged in our bags, dead tired. Desperate sleep came none too soon.

A little after five I started a pot of coffee and walked through the house, double-checking bundles of money to allay nagging doubts. I went out to stretch my legs on the deck. The sage was rife, carried by puffs of wind. The entire Arizona sky was covered in twisting clouds of brilliant fuchsias. I sat back in an Adirondack chair with a steaming mug and began stewing over the bikers and their money. We couldn't exactly roll into Bako and toss the bundles at the doorstep of the Red Hawks' clubhouse. Could we mail it with an insured post just to get the stink off of us? Or turn it in to ATF and tell them we want immunity?

The phone jangled. That'll wake up Liz, I thought. I shot through the door. *Who would call us here?* Who knows our number? The second ring jarred the still living room. In all the commotion, I hadn't even written it down or set it to memory myself. Should I answer it? I reached it just before the third ring could register.

"Hello."

"Is this Gary?" A woman's voice, woven with familiarity.

"Yeah, who's this?" I sounded hostile.

"Gary, this is Karen, your rental agent? I'm sorry to phone so early but I have an appointment on the north side of town that I have to get to soon. Are you going to be home for the next half hour or so?" I heard Liz moving around the back room.

I sat down. "Yeah, yeah, why—what's up?"

"Well, it's something we should talk about in person. Don't be alarmed or anything, but it is important. I can be at your place in, say, twenty minutes or so. Is that okay?"

"Yeah, I guess so," I said, "but no hint, huh?"

"Waa-ell, I'll just talk to you when I get there. I think it's best."
Her voice sounded a little off balance, a measure from the confidence she'd spoken with in the office.

As I reset the handset, Liz pulled open the bedroom door and tiptoed toward me penguin-style, arms thrust against her chilled torso.

"Hug," she whispered, and I hung my arms around her. "Who was that on the phone?"

"Karen, the agent. Said she's coming by to tell us something," I said.

"Right now?"

"Twenty minutes."

Liz turned from my arms and whirled off to the bedroom in a flurry of making the bed. She had, in minutes, straightened the place, slipped into jeans, and was fast applying makeup at the vanity. I brought her coffee.

Not long after Liz emerged from the bedroom in snug jeans and a t-shirt, Karen's Mercedes made a gravelly sound outside the front door. I opened it to a different sky, one where the clouds had broken up. A distant pink horizon had given way to pastel blues.

With sunglasses nested in her hair and a notebook under her arm, Karen slipped past me for the living room. She handed out obligatory compliments on the place, its upkeep, a framed painting of a sailboat caught in rough waters. Liz had bought it downtown. I waved Karen to the sofa and noticed Liz. Her face was lined with worry. The last place I remember seeing her look like that was at the Carrizo Plain.

"So, what's the news, Karen?" I asked.

She pursed her lips and rocked her neck forward as though she'd rehearsed a speech. "Well, I wanted to come in person to tell you what I know because I worried about you two. You're my clients, and I care about—"

Liz flipped open her hand in Karen's direction, cutting her off. "What is it?"

I noticed the expensive perfume of Karen's again. "It's the FBI," she blurted out.

"The FBI?" I asked. "What about 'em?"

Karen's age spots were showing in the light of the house and she kept pursing her lips. "Tracy down at the Monte Vista—the three of you met before?"

I dropped my chin. "Yeah, we know her."

"Anyway, she called me because she gave you my card as a reference."

"Right," I said. "What about her?"

"She said the FBI came in and showed her photographs of you two. They wanted to know if she knew where you were staying, how you could be reached."

"Oh, man."

"And Tracy said that you were guests but had checked out and that she had no idea where you went, which is the truth. She didn't know where you went, but she did tell me that she liked you two the first night you met. She called you 'a cute couple' and all this kind of thing."

"What kind of photos did they show her? Did she say?"

"Well," she paused, with a shifty glance toward Liz, "they had this picture of you, Gary, from your work as a policeman. You know, secret agent job, a picture like that." I wasn't going to bother with correcting her. I knew it was my credential photograph that they had. "And, Liz, were you, you know, ever in jail?"

"Yeah, but it's been a long time," she said.

"Well, the FBI agent had that," she said, biting her lip. "So, anyway, Tracy called me and told me, and that's why I'm here."

I stood up, looking through the picture window and studied the fringe of clouds. I sighed, "So they're looking for us."

Karen stood up and dangled her keys behind me. "Now, just so you know, I'm bound by my employer and by law to reveal to them your rental agreement if they come to me. I can't hide you, in other words," she said, "I could lose my license."

My hands were on my hips as I studied her. She looked at me blankly. "Yeah, I know you can't guard us from the law, Karen. I get it. But, tell me this, then. We're here on a month-to-month, and we have—what number day is this, the 22nd? Okay, so we have eight days left in this house, correct?"

She lowered her face, and her voice took on a hopeful lilt. "That's right, eight days. Are you—are you thinking of moving on? I mean, we could work something out with the owners, you know, get your deposit mailed to you."

"Moving out, yes, but the deposit thing? That's no good," I said and plopped into the sofa, wrestling a throw pillow under my arm. "If I give you a forwarding address, the agents will force you by law to give it to them. See, you won't have a choice in it. I need to sever all connections, so just let me think about that part."

Liz looked around the room. "We'll leave the place spotless, Karen."

"I think in light of the circumstances the owners might work with you. They're very nice people," she said. Her face glowed, and she said with a clap, "And I have a showing to get to for now, so let me see what I can do." She was through the door and down the driveway in minutes.

I turned to Liz. "Well, we got to come up with a plan. I am curious about that rally, if the Red Hawks are coming here."

"Well, I'm not," she said. "Look, this is bad news for us. All of it." The house grew still. I sat staring at the Arizona travel magazine on the end table. Liz sat poised at the sofa's end. She sat up and waved her arms at the ceiling. "We need to get out. I can't live like this! Damn it, we didn't do anything wrong."

A thought came to me, among many crossing wires. I turned to her and slouched over for the tips of her fingers. "Hear me out, okay? Now we know we can't go back to Fresno. And Bakersfield's out, too. And you're right about the biker rally. I go down there and get spotted somehow, that will only prime the pump. Those guys will trail me back here. Plus I got no gun, and I can't get one without even more trouble.

"And on top of it all, here's this real estate agent, telling us that the FBI is closing in."

"Right," she nodded, her face squinted with agreement.

"There's one place I can think of that makes sense on every front, a place where we'll feel safe, that we can go to."

"Yeah, what place is that?"

"Akron."

CHAPTER SEVEN

There were no delays in leaving Arizona. No naps, no hikes to sentimental vista points. Before ten that morning, we'd packed the suitcases, phoned Karen's office with our plan to vacate the home, and slid the key under a flagstone near the stoop. The secretary taking the message seemed to know all about us and sounded more than a little pleased that we were leaving.

I trotted out to the idling car and we roared out of there in a cloud of butterscotch. My belt bag was intact and Liz's purse sat at her feet, freighted with bundles of cash. Route 180 nosed us toward the Grand Canyon, which felt like we'd rolled north to another planet. Its vastness, violent cliffs, and colors brought me to the point of a cold sweat. After all, how many shades of red stone were there?

Liz wanted to keep moving. We knew Interstate 40 was out. That highway would mark us as easy targets for state troopers or bikers out for blood, so we steered north and began the long journey east. We went flying past an Indian reservation and slowed through a national forest, before clearing hellacious grades into Utah. Our car nearly overheated on the climb.

Bryce National Park fed into Piute County and vast reaches of blue space. Driving northward into the teeming Mormon town, we rumbled to a dusty stop in front of an A-frame restaurant with high reaching windows neglected in layers of dirt.

A big brunette with bright red lips set Cokes on the table and then two platters swallowed by giant Buffalo burgers. She slung a hand on the booth and asked where we were from. Liz chatted along while I sat there chewing and staring at the sapphire waters of the Great Salt Lake.

In the morning Liz insisted we see the Salt Lake Desert, a short distance to the west. I mistook the salt blanket for snow that formed its own crust. After several miles into the desert, I slowed and turned the car around, remarking that we could say that we'd seen it. Then we raced for Wyoming and the old Arapaho lands of Vedauwoo, rocky outcrops and rounded cliffs. Signs for Cheyenne, a sprawling western town, called us to an uneventful lunch and another tank of gas. We were soon back on the road, determined to make Denver that night.

A painted sign shouting "WELCOME TO COLORFUL COLO-RADO" greeted us at the state line, its salmon red lettering inside a rustic wooden pole frame. The car hummed along natural boundaries, skirting the southbound ridge that gives form to the Rocky Mountains. Through the passenger window was the great range, immobile and silent. We roared toward Denver, considered taking the outer belt north to Kansas to make time, but she'd never been to Denver. So we hooked onto a ramp into town.

Huddled together, great rail yards converged for the play of freight cars marked 'South Pacific' and 'Burlington Northern Santa Fe.' Tracks stretched and squeezed in parallel lines, others split in subtle degrees in and out of Denver. We crossed some tracks to a stout brick building painted white with dull green awnings.

A wiry blonde with baggy eyes skirted over to us. I imagined she'd smoked cigarettes since diapers. She poured coffee with controlled splashes and looked up at us. I chafed my hands together, tugged at a Giants ball cap I'd thrown on, and looked around: rail workers coming off a shift, ruddy skinned in dirty dungarees.

"What do you have," the old waitress declared without pause. A laminated menu appeared from under the counter.

"Uh," I sighed.

"We ain't got any of that," she said, cracking her gum. I smiled and got a fix on the sandwich specials.

Liz cleared her throat. "I'll take your tuna sandwich with a Coke, hold the chips." I could hear a pencil scratching it down.

"I guess I'll just take some of your tomato soup . . . a bowl," I said.

She flipped the pad in her palm with a dirty white pencil. "Crackers?"

I glanced around. "Butter, too," I reminded her.

In a whirl, she snapped the small sheet from the pad and clipped it to the order tray above the pass through. "Tuna sand, no chip. Splash of red noise with a butter float," she said and sauntered off in soft-soled shoes.

"Sheesh," I muttered in Liz's ear, "not exactly the Village Inn, is it?"

Liz grinned and rubbed my thigh. At counter's end a guy wearing a Mack cap pulled low and a jean jacket worked his toothpick. The waitress leaned in close to him and hummed something indistinguishable. I sipped coffee and studied the atlas I'd spread over the counter. "Look at this, Liz. Says here the population of Cheyenne is just 22,000. That's crazy. A city as old as Cheyenne and nothing more than Cuyahoga Falls?"

"What's Cuyahoga Falls?"

I sniffed at that. "It's just a little town, a suburb of Akron. But the doings of Cheyenne could run the entire state of Wyoming, half a million people. I wonder how many miles of land per person? Hmm." I flipped to the index as Blondie arrived with a charger of soup. I studied the breadth of Kansas, its tiny towns marking select roads, careful not to spill from the bowl. When the soup and sandwich were gone and the map was studied, we left through the worn door with the atlas under my arm.

"Grandma?" I yelled into the pay phone outside the diner. Liz stood next to me, her eyes bright with excitement. "It's me, Gary. I'm coming back, Grandma. Back to Akron. Yep, to live. For good. And I got a new girlfriend I want you to meet. Her name's Liz . . . yes. Yes. And she looks like one of them girls in the magazines."

Liz rolled her eyes, and a semi roared up the street.

"Yeah, Grandma, it'll be a few days yet. We're just now in Denver. Right. We'll see you then." I hung up with a grin.

Liz stood there, anxious. "What'd she say?"

"She's funny. She just hangs up, never says 'goodbye,'" I said. "She can't wait to meet you. I think you'll like her. A lot. Everybody but my mom does."

"I bet I will," she said, swinging open her door. I swung through the city and found a joint downtown where we spent the noisiest night of the trip.

On the prairies of Kansas, we found an Indian burial ground along a good stretch of empty interstate. A shoddy billboard with a chieftain's bust called in tourists. And there, collecting a fee from tourists to view huddled bones unearthed and slopped with browning varnish, sat one miserable son of a bitch. I pressed into the man's hand two dollars to walk through his billowing canvas tent. One old woman wearing a rain bonnet stepped between grave sites, looking down at bones of women and children, maybe a chief, shaking her head and making a tsk-tsk sound between her teeth. Liz studied the old woman.

I wondered aloud how it might feel for the melon-bellied proprietor if his own kin were dragged to light like this, exhumed for the sake of four quarters from a stranger's pocket. We left the tent complaining.

The Great Plains proved redundant: more waving wheat than I had ever imagined, a tractor groaning through a muddy thoroughfare, and a shaky crop duster flying low. The taped cassettes had all been played, some more than once. But the motor forced the miles aside and Liz and I moved on to another little town for the night.

There at a plateau stood a hillside hotel with a sign for food. A vendor in the lobby sold fresh sandwiches and Sarsaparilla on ice. I took one of the cold brown bottles and squeezed its cap with a turn. We sat in big soft leather chairs in the lobby, where gas light flickered inside a stone fireplace. It was overshadowed by a gigantic buffalo head mounted on the wall.

As I chewed, I raised the bottle. "You going to call your dad?" I asked with a burp. "Pardon."

"Yeah, I need to see what's going on."

While she squeezed into an old-fashioned phone booth, I stared through the window into the waving prairie. My thoughts zoomed ahead to Akron, its likely lake weather.

"What'd you find out?" I asked as she plopped down and turned the sandwich for a bite.

"Nothing, really. Dad said Rex hasn't heard anything, and his teeth are fixed, but he'll have a scar along his lip line." She raised her elbows with a shrug.

"I still can't believe they came after him because of what we did."

She sniffed and rolled her tongue over her teeth. "Welp, I told you, Stan had a lot of power. He wasn't just a meth cook, he was the best in Kern County, maybe in all of California."

"The King. Well, maybe they'll leave your family alone for now," I said.

"I don't know," she said.

"We should send your brother a money order for the cost of his dental work and then some. You know, go into a post office, buy one for a thousand bucks, and send it to him."

She sat up and folded the sandwich wrapper. "Could we? I mean, that would mean so much to me. You have no idea how bad I feel about my brother."

"Absolutely," I said, standing and brushing off crumbs. "Let's do it."

CHAPTER EIGHT

At first light I rose to work out. Outside I broke a sweat running through drizzle on a dull, dark bridge that crossed the Missouri River into Kansas City. Back at the room I waited for Liz in the hotel shower. Afterward, we dressed for cold rains and were on the road again, warmed in the car's heater fan. Hours into Missouri, we took in Columbia's museum, holding hands and staring at paintings centered on war, a collection of broad grotesque figures. Men with steel pots on their heads running bayonets through some other poor soldiers. The gallery enveloped my thoughts about ATF—carrying a gun, killing Gorman at the cabin—or ATF enveloped my thoughts about the gallery, I wasn't sure. The buzz of museum lights went silent. I even forgot my highway bearing, that velocitized sensation that hits me on exit ramps.

"You okay?"

"Huh?"

"Are you okay?" Liz repeated, her face in my line of vision.

"Uh, yeah," I said. I shook the act of murder from my mind and forced a smile. "I was just checking out these soldiers."

"Well," she said with a squeeze of my hand, "you told me at the ocean, you don't want to feel like a soldier for the President anymore, right?"

"Yes, I did say that." I slipped my arm around her waist and hugged her in the gallery. An older woman who'd identified herself as a curator stood in the distance with her arms crossed. I waved my arms at the Benton paintings. "It was just the paintings," I called to her. She made a sallow face and disappeared. It was time to motor onto the next state, I told Liz.

The air outside a drizzly Illinois restaurant smelled damp and greasy. Gray pitted puddles formed plate-sized moon craters where an old wet Chevy truck rested in the parking space next to us. In the cramped booth, I ordered veal and potatoes and thumbed through pages of the Atlas. An elderly man hanging a gray scarf around his neck in the next booth smiled as I finished. I acknowledged the man and summoned the waitress for our bill. Liz had gone to the ladies' room.

"I see you're travelers," the old man began. "Going far?"

"Yeah," I answered, "Ohio. It's a 12-hour day for us. Come from Kansas City last night."

He ran his hand through his gray clipped hair. "Ah, Ohio. That's not too far. I got a sister in Ohio, lives in Bellefontaine."

I fumbled for change to match the number on the ticket and a few dollars for the waitress. "That's a long way from where I am. I'm on the eastern side south of Cleveland."

"So, what do you keep in that?" He was studying my beltline, the cash bag.

I froze. My first words coughed up all wrong. "None of your business."

He raised his hands. "Ah, no offense. I've seen men wearing those pouches these days. I just wondered if you cared for it, that was all."

My hand was hot on the food bill and I tapped the pouch. "Some guys put their keys in there, a driver's license, small stuff." The old man looked far away for a second. I told him to take care and moved away.

"Well, good luck to you," he choked at a whisper. I stood in line at the register and glanced at him sitting there, looking emptier than he had before.

* * *

At the Indianapolis racetrack we got on a little diesel bus, making a circle before its enormous grandstand. Inside the museum, browsing brilliant yellow and blue roadsters, Porsches, and old surreys, I felt pressed to keep moving, slightly claustrophobic about getting home.

Leaning over the partition rope, I marveled at twin cylinders of a vintage Indian, one motorcycle so old it resembled a Whizzer. "These are pretty cool," I said.

"Would you ever ride one?" she asked, jostling me. Her perfume was heavy from the damp day but still had a magical smell going back to the California plain of flowers.

"I don't know. Why?"

I felt her shiver with excitement. She had her hair pulled tight off her face in a 50s-style ponytail with a white ribbon and tiny pearl earrings. She looked good. "It might be fun to go riding together."

"What, like you and Stanley?"

"Pardon me?"

"Uh—I didn't mean that."

She studied me, her upturned lip showing a mischievous side. "Well, I can't go on poker runs with a dead man, now, can I?"

"Oh, man," I said, "you are brutal. But it was still a lousy thing to say . . . I'm sorry." I laid a hand at the small of her lower back as we left the museum. Getting into the worn seats of the car, Liz handed me a tape of Dwight Yoakam songs. I drove off and she sang along.

"How come you never sang for me before?" I asked.

She shook her head. "Time wasn't right. Singing for somebody's personal," she said, bopping her head and returning to the next refrain. The motor hummed up the ramp to the highway as we rolled across eastern counties of the state.

And there on the horizon awaited my state's banner, Ohio's highway of welcome. "We made it," I announced and Liz kissed my cheek. Eventually, Columbus came into view as motorists burrowed along through the city. The big road, I-70, sprang from

the southwest side of Columbus into a horrible intersection of
highways, each ramp and road lapped over by a series of ugly
and magnificent bridges. Large tractor-trailer rigs whooshed and
belched past us.

I finished the tangle of highways and aimed the car toward
Cleveland. I stared at coffee swirling like walnut dye in the cup.
My mouth felt dry and black. So I sipped the water and studied the
imperfect roads, I-71's cracks and erratic tar lines while gleaming
automobiles glided past. The sound of the road dried to a hum and
Pink Floyd's music dripped to a melancholy end, the final notes
riding over the silence between songs. I cracked the tape from the
player, fumbled its return to a case, and glanced at Liz.

"I'm bored of riding. But I can't wait to see your hometown,"
she said, "just to see how you grew up. I mean, you know so much
about my background."

"Bottom line," I said, raising my finger, "is that we're both
hillbillies from different parts of the country. Here they call us
Rednecks, out there they call you Okies."

She pursed her lips and stared out the window. "Well, I don't
especially care for that term."

"Good people are good people," I said with a shake of my head,
"the place you live can't make it for you."

Around the bend onto 76 toward Barberton were few cars.
Night drank in the road as the soft blue evening dimmed. Land
opened to hills west of Rittman, sloped away from the storm crest
of Lodi, and the car hummed faster, anxious.

* * *

A nosy front desk clerk at the Holiday Inn in Fairlawn wanted to
know what had brought us to Akron. Before dropping my license
to the counter, I considered answering the question "I murdered
some guys," but I shrugged instead and winked at Liz. "We're just
coming back home from a long drive across the country. That's all."

"Oh," the redhead answered. "That sounds fun, kind of adven-
turous, too."

"Oh, it's been an adventure alright," Liz said with a giggle. Pulling our bags into the room, I sat on the bed with a telephone receiver in my hand. The phone at my grandma's house was ringing. Into its third ring, it broke off.

"Hello?" a voice asked.

"Robin?"

"Hi," she answered, "how's it going?"

"Robin?"

"Yeah, where are you?" She breathed through the line in a normal rhythm.

"I'm in Akron. What are you doing at my grandma's?" I crabbed. Liz swept into the bedroom area from the bathroom, an eyeliner wand in her fingertips, her face marked with concern. I covered the speaker and mouthed *Robin*. Liz plopped down at the bed's edge, her face blank.

"I came over for a visit, you know, catching up on olden days," Robin said.

"Well, put my grandma on, will you?" The phone felt hot in my hand and I shifted hands, even thought to hang up on her. When my grandmother came to the line, I kept it short. We'd be over tomorrow. And we would not want her there. My grandma agreed and left the line.

I replaced the receiver and dropped back to the bed. The room grew silent. I breathed out. Liz returned to the bathroom and I heard her mumble, "Wow. Welcome home, Gary."

CHAPTER NINE

I woke well rested. I dressed in the quiet. I noticed by stepping into the hotel parking lot and looking westward, blue shades of the sky had become steely. And it was chilly out. But it felt good, an Ohio metallic cold. Absent from the air were agricultural dust and desert sage. I squatted a little in the parking lot to see how the car dipped from weight of luggage and went back in.

The smell of human warmth blended with the hotel room's chalky paint and bleached sheets. The rise and fall of Leslie's breast formed a silhouette across the dimly lit bed. The coffee maker in the bathroom I flipped to off. A large pizza box I crushed and dumped with it an empty bottle of red. Celebratory voices from the night before echoed.

Liz rose and dressed and we headed for the cramped and crowded apartments of southeast Akron, where my grandmother patronized Arlington Plaza daily for milk or bread. It was a worry of mine, her rubbing shoulders with welfare cheats, street punks, and white trash. All the old families had gone. Somehow still, she enjoyed a halo of protection. I eased down Virginia Avenue from Wilbeth Road and pointed out boyhood haunts, the telephone pole where I had pulled a fire alarm, a speed ramp where we had wrecked bicycles.

"Grandma? It's me, Gary," I called at the door. Liz stood behind me, her ponytail tied with a white scarf. She wore a cotton sundress flecked with floral prints. "You look good this morning," I whispered, "that dress is smoking." Waiting for footsteps within the apartment, I reached behind Liz and rubbed her rounded backside, catching a panty line with my fingertips.

She batted my hand away. "Gary," she whimpered, "not now. I'm here to meet your grandma."

The door creaked open and there stood my silver-haired grandmother. "Hello, Gary."

"Grandma!" I hugged her shoulders. They were still muscled from garden labor. The facial sagging had come by way of age and gravity, but her appearance attested to a distant youthful beauty. I'd seen pictures of her in flapper girl dresses, the waxy curls poised along her cheeks.

"Oh, look who's come back home," she sang, stepping back into the tiny living room. "Let me look at you." She pounded my shoulder. Her hair was set and curled, wise owl plastic frames perched on her nose. Her house smelled of bacon and on the window's ledge I saw a row of beefsteak tomatoes.

I pulled back and turned to Liz. "Grandma, this is the love of my life, Leslie Harlan."

"Leslie, it's nice to meet you."

"It's a pleasure, ma'am."

I heard the reluctance in my grandmother's voice. *Not your wife.* I put a hand on my grandma's shoulder. "Her people are from Bakersfield by way of Oklahoma."

"Oh, them's good people," she said. "Now, you fers come on in and have a seat. I just read the table and was making a bite to eat for you since Gary said you was coming this morning." We gathered around the table in her oversized chairs while my grandma sliced tomatoes and snapped the toaster down for BLT sandwiches. Her Bible had been marked with a silk band and left open.

"Revelations, huh, Grandma?"

"It's all in there, what's about to happen."

I leaned over it and scanned a couple verses. "I wish I knew," I said, glancing at Liz. On the table in front of us sat a serving bowl swimming with cucumber salad, its vinegar pungent and sweetened with sugar. "Grandma, this looks good."

"Got fresh coffee here," she said, pouring from the same perco-lator pot she'd had since the '60s. The room steamed with buttery flavors. "And I'll have you fers sandwiches in just a minute."

Liz watched my grandma's flurry of hands at pans in the sink. "Is there anything I can do, ma'am?"

Over my shoulder, my grandmother corrected Liz. "No, you can just sit and visit. Oh, you can call me 'Grandma'. Some say 'Whitey' for short. You say your family name's Harlan?" Grandma asked.

Liz nodded. "Yes, it is."

"That's a mite funny 'cause we knew a family of that eponym when I was just a girl growing up in Summersville."

Liz shook her head. "No, ma'am, my family's all from Craig County near Vinita. It's in the northeast corner of Oklahoma. We're mostly Irish, I think, Scots-Irish."

Grandma set the sandwiches on plates with bowls for salad, and I passed Liz the serving bowl. My sandwich was gone in a matter of minutes, the salad, too. To my left, my grandma slurped at the hot coffee and studied me.

"Eating like you ain't seen food, Gary," Grandma laughed and looked at Liz.

"I'm hungry. Not too much home cookin' on the road. Liz here's a good cook, though."

"Well," she said with a nervous grin at Liz, "that's good. That's fine." I could see in her eyes something was wrong. I wiped my mouth and sat back, folding my napkin across my thigh.

"Well, Grandma," I began, "I know you had a visitor yesterday, so out with it. You might as well spill it. And while we're at it, Liz knows all about Robin, so what you say to me you can say to her as well." Liz put her sandwich down and wiped her mouth.

Grandma grew quiet, her head tipped, eyes working the corners of the ceiling. "Well, let me see. She come running up just before it took to pouring down the rain. And naturally, I had her in and made her something to eat. I was glad for the company, you might expect, so I made us roasting ears and a mess of beans, and we started out right, just like times back when you'd bring her around."

There was a drag in her voice.

"Then what happened?"

"Well, then you called and talked to her," she said. "She come off the phone and says to me, 'I can't believe he's come back to Akron. He's got some nerve.'"

I smirked. "She said that? Then what?"

Grandma's eyes grew glassy. I glanced at Liz, who was studying her. "Well now, here's the thing. I don't care much for quarreling, and I don't want you flying off the handle when I tell you this bit."

"Grandma," I said, "just tell me."

She slumped and set the coffee down and began folding her napkin. It reminded me of Smith's Bakery out in Bakersfield when Liz and I did that half the time we were talking. "She'd been drinking. Set here and tell me she had it under check and on and on thataway. From your granddad on, I can spot a drunk a mile away. Smelled like she'd just been to the bag store."

"What's the bag store?" Liz asked.

I leaned in. "State store. Package store, whatever." Then I turned back to Grandma. "So, she was here and had been drinking. Then what?"

"Well, she started in on you first, Gary. Said she wanted nothing better than to beat the fire out of you for what happened in Fresno. Said she was bad off out there, and you wouldn't so much as call the doctor."

I laughed. "She said that? When I told her we'd get her counseling for it, she hung up on me! God dang drunk. Sorry, Grandma, but that ain't how it was."

"I know, I know. Hear me out now," she said with a cautious hand. "So, she said them fellas you worked for out there, they come to her house when you was a fur piece from home." I noticed my grandma was back to talking to the napkin. "They said you wasn't answering your radio calls."

She winced at Liz and paused. "Said you'd run off with a strange woman—I'm just repeating, mind. That's what she claim they told her. So, I set here and listened and she teared up, come apart in a crying jag. But I got her calmed down to get her to render the rest." Her eyes went back to Liz. "I can see you ain't a rough woman."

Liz smiled. I covered her hand with mine.

"So, she went on with it. Said they told her there was trouble up in the mountains. That you fers run off with all her husband's money, something such as that."

"Hold on, Grandma. There's a whole other side," I said. "First of all, Liz isn't even married and that guy—"

Liz raised her hand from the table. "It's okay. Let her finish." The two exchanged an understanding smile. I could just see Robin's sloppy grin, sitting here half-drunk spewing half-truths.

My grandma cleared her throat. "Now then, she said they told her the husband come after his wife and the money but you shot him down, killed him and another fella deader'n a hammer."

I shook my head at what I was hearing. "Is that it?"

The napkin was unfolded and pressed, refolded and back again. "She said you bought yourself a brand-spanking new car with some of that money, and that the law was trying to trace you down out there." A hush fell over the kitchen.

I took a deep breath, let it out, and put my face in my hands. I snickered, running my fingers through my hair, peeking out at her nervous, flickering eyes. "Alright, Grandma," I said, "I'll work backwards and tell you the truth about everything you heard from her." I opened my hands. "First of all, she lied about the car. It's a used Honda, not a new car. Secondly, the man that I killed I shot in self-defense. He came after us when we were in a mountain cabin. He and another biker came after us with guns and they tried to kill both of us. And I know, *Thou shall not kill,* that's one of the Commandments. And after it was over, I sat on the porch and looked at that man's body lying there, and I remembered what you said all those times."

"Oh, dear," she said, placing her hand at her heart.

"Grandma, I know, but I didn't have a choice. They came after us," I swore. "Frankly, I shouldn't be telling you any of this because I don't want you a party to my mess.

"But, that money we took was money he was using to buy drugs with. On top of it, he'd abused Liz here for years, so she felt she had the money coming to her. So we took it. But most of all, the two of us just wanted out of that Valley. It wasn't like we took his retirement from working for years at the Children's Home.

"But this story you heard. You know that's Robin being Robin. Also for the record, Liz was never married to that man. And yeah, I left my job and didn't answer calls, but I turned in all of my equipment and tendered them a letter of resignation.

"Now, those are the facts." I sighed and started laughing, louder and louder. "Robin. Oh, dear Robin and her stories." I turned to Liz. "See what I mean? She comes over to my own grandma's drunk and spreads lies to my own family."

Grandma spoke up. "I knew there wasn't a bit of truth in it. Of course, I worried terrible about you." Her face stirred with lines of age.

"I know you did, Grandma. So, what's she doing with herself since she's back in town?"

"Well, when she first come in here, she was just as proud as could be, going on about how she was gonna take up nursing down there at the university this fall. I asked about you and she told me you fers was separated and that it was through—"

"Did she mention getting a divorce at all?"

"She did. Said she's been taking up with another man, real big fella from Firestone. She said he's got muscles on top of muscles, and I said, 'well, he can't be bigger than Gary.' And she said he's a bodybuilder and he goes in for those muscle shows."

"That's Raff. I know him. He's an okay guy," I said. "I used to see him up at Bodybuilder's. He's a big guy alright, and I knew he always liked her. She'd tease me about him. Well, now he can have her with my blessing."

My grandma furrowed her brow and rose for the coffee pot, topping off our mugs and passing Liz the sugar bowl. "Now then, you know how I feel about marriage under the Church. You want to watch what you say. That's still your wife in the eyes of the Lord."

I yielded an open hand. "No, you're right, Grandma. I just want to be through with Robin is all."

She sat back down. She looked at me with hard eyes. "Now I want you to tell me something, the both of you." She glanced at Leslie. "You two been together?"

"*Grandma.*"

"Yes or no."

"I don't want to answer that question," I said.

I felt Leslie's hand squeeze mine as she leaned over the table. "Yes, Grandma, we have. And you should know we're in love, just like Gary said. And just so you know, I've only ever been with one other man." I looked at my grandma for a reaction.

She dipped her chin. "Now you two want to come by it honest before you turn up pregnant. That'll keep 'em all from talking. Now you go get that Bible divorce just as soon as you fers get yourselves a place and set up housekeeping. Then make an honest woman of this one. I can see she's good." Her eyes twinkled and I felt at that very second that Liz was warm for my grandma.

I rubbed my chin. "We're going over this afternoon to Highland Square to look at a brownstone apartment. I called on a Beacon ad just this morning from the hotel." Then I turned to Liz. "And if that works out—you don't know this yet—I want to take you to Luigi's, best pizza joint in the city. We'll celebrate tonight."

My grandma's face was all business. "That's fine. Now what's all this about the money?"

I flipped up my hands with a grin. "It's out in the car, locked in the trunk. Eighty grand, Grandma. You want a loan?"

She shook her head. "You get rid of that money. You figure out a way. That's the devil's money. You want some proof, you just read the sixth chapter of Leviticus. It ain't no good for you tainting a new courtship thataway. You was raised to know better."

"Easier said than done, Grandma. Everywhere I go—banks, car dealers, realtors—you can't give them money without declaring it to the federal government."

She ceased folding the napkin and cleared her throat, her blue eyes glassy and true. "That money's bad now, comes from broken folks. You send it back to them with a fifth added on top. That's the only way in the eyes of the Lord."

"But what if we did something good with it instead? Something really good. Besides, I can't give money back to a guy that . . . well, you know."

I looked at Liz. She was transfixed on my grandmother's face and gave a solemn nod.

* * *

That afternoon Liz and I wandered inside the brownstone, gazing at its hardwood molding, its doorway heights looming and broad. Small tiled floors with ornate trim covered the kitchen and bathroom floors. The place had a storied smell, a tad dusty. I imagined us getting cool nights of deep sleep on this fourth story of the building. Its back bedroom wrapped around to the rear, where it overlooked an alley and covered parking.

Liz poked around the kitchen, a sheaf of apartment ads pinched between her fingers. When she caught my eye from across the room, I raised my chin at her and opened my palms as if to ask *what do you think?* Her eyes squinted. She nodded and the light of the room shone on her cheeks.

"Uh, ma'am," I called to the agent.

She was tinkering in the other room with the hinge of a trash chute. "Thing needs oiled. I'll write that down for maintenance," she mumbled. Her heels clicked into the empty room. A young blonde woman with a pointy nose that didn't take away from her looks, she was all ballpoint pens and notebooks, her eyes flicking about the place as a home inspector's might. "What do you think, Mr. Whitehall?"

"We'll take it," I said, "and I'll just pay with cash today, first month's and the security deposit."

"Oh, that's just fine," she said. "I can tell the others it's taken. There were two other couples interested."

"Good," I said. At the kitchen counter I peeled off nine $100 bills from a stack of twelve I'd folded in my pocket. Papers were signed and within minutes she was gone. I turned and raised my hands in a great shout. "Back home in Akron!"

Wending from one end of the city to another had an old shoe feel. Unlike Flagstaff, where we had perched ourselves over a stony outcrop at the head of a canyon, our house sat at the rise of Market Street hill. We were no longer vulnerable to desert moons and evil spirits on horseback. I knew the talk of our blended neighborhood, the place situated in a funky village. But the southeast side was still home. There was something familiar about the Arlington Street crazies who had roughed me up as a boy.

After buying a used Impala—a '74 rebuild in leaf-green paint with quarter panels suited for tank construction—I had solid work transportation for just under 1200 bucks. I returned to Thrall's landscaping crew to work for cash under the table, all without filling out a single piece of paper.

It was simple. Show up at seven-thirty weekday mornings when it didn't rain, jump on the stake truck heaped high with mulch, and ride out to Fairlawn or Bath. I spent each day with a pitchfork in gloved hands. I'd wheel the mulch alongside some sprawling colonial place, fling it in small piles, and down to my knees to spread it. And on Friday afternoons, I'd collect a modest wad of cash. It was just a couple bucks over minimum wage, but I imposed on no one and no one was after me.

Liz was even luckier. A girl with whom I'd gone to high school managed a restaurant in the Valley, a swanky affair in Carnaby Street Commons. The place was well known for its steaks and seafood, its top-shelf cocktails. Original art hung on the walls. When I phoned Rhonda to ask if she had an opening for servers, she seemed wary. Who was I trying to help land a job?

Images of Liz working the Village Inn reeled through my mind. Figuratively speaking, she had owned that place, the customers had loved her. I assured Rhonda that, if given the chance to prove herself, my California girlfriend would show her that she would be the lucky one. The catch, I coughed up, was that Liz needed the job without an employee packet being run. Could she just show up and work for cash from the till and tips? I knew it sounded

strange, but we'd run into trouble out West. A reluctant voice told me where Liz should appear for an informal interview.

The first night Liz returned to the apartment with a click of the handle and whoosh of the front door. A bowtie hung skewed from the collar of her formal white shirt. A thick leather-bound menu dangled from her arm. I'd been painting the utility room and set down the brush with a rag in my hands. She looked tired and my first thought was to hug her but I was speckled in paint. A single loveseat and television on a stand, both covered in plastic, separated us in the chaotic room.

"Hello-oo."

"Hi," I sighed, tossing the rag over my shoulder. "How'd the first night go?" I pecked her on the cheek.

"My feet are tired," she said, "and I want to sit down." I lifted the plastic from the loveseat and lowered myself to the floor across from her, leaning against one of the few unpainted walls left in the apartment.

"Talk to me," I said.

"Well," she began, "I liked it. I mean, it's a nice place for starters. The menu's going to take some getting used to—I don't know how many times I had to go back to the kitchen for specifics, but that was to be expected." She raised the menu and let it rest on the seat next to her.

"Your outfit's nice," I said, "kind of upscale."

"Yeah, I suppose so, kind of tight around the neck. I'm used to my apron and blouses at the Village."

I scratched at the paint flecks on my forearm, speckled from the roller. "So, tell me, how was Rhonda? Was she cool?"

"You know, I hardly saw her. Mostly, I shadowed this older woman Grace, but she could see I knew what I was doing. That Grace lady was a riot, walking through the kitchen singing show tunes and gospel hymns, and when the shift was over, she actually skipped to her car. She's hilarious."

"That's cool. So, what'd you make?"

"Well," she said, springing to her feet and fishing into her apron pockets, "I counted forty-eight in tips and Rhonda said she'll give

me another three dollars per hour in cash, so that's . . . times seven
. . . twenty-one and forty-eight."

"Sixty-nine bucks."

"It's not bad," she said with a groan, rubbing her shoulder.

"But seventy bucks in seven hours, that's ten bucks an hour. A
lot better than what I'm making slinging mulch." I rolled my eyes
and twirled the paint rag in the air.

She kicked off her shoes. "Plus, I didn't even get a full shift
because of the shadowing, and on top of it, Grace said Friday and
Saturday nights are when you really make a killing. She said some
nights she'll leave out of there with over a hundred and fifty in tips."

I rose to finish painting before the roller would have a chance
to clot. "You got to work every weekend night?"

"I wish. Grace said for girls just starting, you'll be lucky to get
one of the weekend nights. And when I was leaving, Grace told
Rhonda I was a natural. So, Rhonda asked if I could work Friday
and Sunday night this weekend, and I told her yes."

I shrugged. "I guess that's good. You know, making a living
between us till all this stuff blows over."

* * *

And it did blow over, for the most part. Not long after moving in, I ran
into Robin one evening coming out of Annabelle's Tavern. I'd been
on my way to order sandwiches a couple doors down when she came
bouncing out of the place, her spirits high, saccharine booze on her
breath. It felt strange to me, standing there on Market Street, cars
whizzing past, talking with Robin Whitehall. *My wife.* I felt waves of
goose bumps. My sandwich order could wait, she said, and pulled
my sleeve toward the door of the bar. I owed her at least one drink,
she claimed, so with a foolish shrug, through the door I went.

Sitting in an empty bar with metal music too loud to converse,
I watched Robin debase herself, slipping by degrees into further
drunkenness over a monster margarita. Granules of salt clinging to
her lips, she waved off my need to run. I kept looking at the steel
door and gesturing with my thumb. She dismissed it and bragged
how I still wanted to be with her, she just knew it. She could just

feel it, she slurred. Her attitude, the slobber at her lips, all of it, brought me to my feet.

I turned to Robin and glared in her eyes. She looked guilty, shifting to a downward glaze as I spoke. "Why would you go over to my grandma's house and make all that stuff up, huh? My own grandma?"

She looked away but I leaned in and hissed, "You got a lot of nerve. You made it sound like I was some criminal on the run. After everything you did to wreck the marriage? I don't suppose you mentioned to her how you drank around the clock out there without a break, did you? You couldn't even stand up straight half the time. And look at you now." I slapped the bar with cash. "You drag me in here like you're on the set in some Hollywood movie and—"

Her hands were on my shoulders and chest. The song ended. It grew quiet in the place. "Can't you see why? Can't you figure it out?"

"What?"

"I—I wanted . . . I—I," she stammered, tapping her fingertips over my chest.

I shook loose of her hands. "Spit it out for God's sake."

"I still love you."

New music shook me. "Are you serious? How drunk are you?" I asked, closely checking her customary droopy lids. I slipped from her finger's grip of my shirt sleeve, leaving a ten for the disinterested bull of a man poring over a magazine at the far end. As I turned to leave, Robin was right behind me and I bumped into her. She teetered, a drunkard's wobble right out of our California apartment. I had to catch her from falling off her heels and when I did, she embraced me, her face buried against my neck. It sickened me, the feel of her body against mine. I righted her posture, patted her back, those wild eyes spinning at me on a fantasy ride. And with a firm release, I stepped for the door and into the street.

Behind me the sound of heels clicked across the walk. That's when she pleaded for a lift home, whining and groping at my arms. I stood there shaking my head, in the public eye with a woman I wanted nothing to do with, the front window of our apartment just down the street. I made Robin promise to meet me in the bar's back parking lot. Then I trotted home, fired up the car, and wheeled around to pick her up.

The ride to her parents' home down Merriman Road was uneventful. Some awkward chitchat passed between us, and then I was pulling up to the house. She purred how no one was home, that she had the place all to herself. I looked in her eyes and drifted back years, remembering in watercolors how she once was.

* * *

"What the hell is this?" Liz wanted to know, studying lipstick marks on my neck as I removed two steak sandwiches from a grease-spotted paper bag.

"Robin."

"Robin? Are you serious?"

"Yeah, I'm serious," I said and bobbed in agreement, "I just saw her across the street. It was nothing." I brought down two plates from the stiff cupboard.

Liz crossed her arms and flipped the hair she'd been blow drying from her face. That gesture always captured me. "So," she began with an aggravated tone, "let me get this straight. You were somewhere with your wife and she kissed you, and it 'was nothing'? That's how it happened?"

"That's about right."

"Where were you?"

"Annabelle's."

She grunted at me as I unwrapped my sandwich and held a glass beneath the kitchen faucet. "So, you two were drinking together, too? This is making my heart beat hard."

I twisted the faucet handle to a drip and turned toward Liz, the sandwich plate in one hand, a glass of water in the other. She stood between me and the loveseat. "Come here," I said, stepping in, "smell my breath." Liz made a sour face but complied and I breathed in her face. "You see? I didn't drink with her. I didn't want to be with her. She said I owed her a drink, and I bought her one, and I sat there watching her get drunk in an empty bar. It was a real turn on. And she got drunk, and I paid out, and when I turned to leave, she stumbled, and I grabbed her and she . . . wrapped herself around me, and I pressed her back and left. And that's the honest truth."

I circled Liz, her fists planted on her hips, eyes blue and sharp. "She 'wrapped herself' around you? And, what's this bit, you owed her a drink?"

"Yeah, something like that," I said, sitting and taking the steak sandwich in both hands. "She almost fell over, and I kept her from falling. That's how drunk she was."

Liz had turned toward me, taking a seat in the new armchair. She sat and folded her hands. "And I'm supposed to believe that?"

I leaned down, supplicating before the food got cold. Her eyes were bright and glaring for an answer when my prayer ended. "I don't care if you believe it or not," I said, "it's the truth. Like I told you in California, I'm through lying to you. To anybody, for that matter." I crunched into the sandwich bread, the rich tasting meat, chewing and looking at Liz.

"Well, that's a terrific attitude," she said, shaking her head at me.

"Truth," I repeated with my mouth full.

CHAPTER TEN

Two months later, on a rainy Friday morning, I called Mr. Thrall on the telephone. I was told to come in, pick up some hours around the shop, clean and oil equipment, and to jump on a truck should the rain blow over. Halfway to the shop, however, it started pouring. The Impala wipers skidded and popped, skidded and popped, each dry swath peppered with rain.

The boss stood under the overhead garage door as I pulled up to the shop, cracking a small vent and leaning back from the dribble of rain. He was shaking his head and yelling something. "Just go back home," he shouted, "we'll try again tomorrow." I whirled the window handle to a damp seal and roared out of there with a wave, for my grandma's down the street.

She'd just set breakfast dishes in a sudsy sink and was sitting down to coffee and the paper when I hurtled for her door. I leapt across the threshold and within minutes was at the kitchen table, sipping coffee, grazing the classifieds, and stroking my wet hair to dry on my palm.

"Hey, Grandma, listen to this," I began, sitting up over the paper. "It's under LAND AND FARMS. Hocking County. 41 acres with cabin and mountain view. Perfect for outdoorsmen. Well on site with propane tank. Two bedroom cabin with full utilities. $65,000 OBO. Now, that sounds pretty good. What a price."

"Hocking County's down there a ways. Pretty country, but you sure you'd want to move again? You fers are just getting settled."

"Yeah, I guess," I said, "but this is a place I could pay cash for, then just wait for the right time to move. I might even surprise Liz with it. I know one thing: She liked that cabin we stayed in when we were in the California mountains. She didn't want to leave that place. Not until—"

"Not until what?"

"Aw, never mind," I said with a slough. "But I might call on this one. It just sounds interesting, and the number's right here." I rose with the paper's ad circled. "Can I use the phone in there?"

She framed her hand around the coffee cup, her light framed glasses down on her nose. "'Course, help yourself."

I moved in for the broad chair with the telephone next to it and dialed the numbers, smiling that she'd refused to update to a push button phone. "Besides," I yelled to her as the numbers rang and chimed in my ear, "not like we're going to become millionaires living here in Akron, with her waitressing and me—hello?"

"Yeah," a dark voice answered.

"Yes, sir. I'm calling about the property you have listed in the paper, up here in Akron?"

"What about it?" the voice crabbed. In the background, machinery screamed then slowed to a dull vibration.

I raised my eyebrows at the receiver. "Well, can you at least tell me about it?"

The machinery kicked back in to a high scream before stopping with a pronounced whine. "Look, son," he shouted through the line, "you want to come down and look at it, fine. You probably don't even know where Hocking County's at. So I'll have to tell you, only for you to tell me you want to think about it. To tell you the truth, I ain't had nothing but headaches since I put that spot in. City people calling, wanting me to tell 'em all about it, on and on. Then I get to the end of it and then they say, 'Well, we got to think about it.' They're just wasting my time, and I got wood in the yard that needs splitting. So, if you want to come down, then come on down, but don't ask me to tell you all about it." The machine was loud again, and the line clicked off.

"Hello?" I asked. Grandma sniggered. "He hung up on me. Son of a—what kind of guy is this?"

"Hillbilly," Grandma said, "didn't want to fool with it."

"Yeah, but when you're trying to sell something to somebody, sheesh." I flipped the paper open to the blue circle once more and redialed the number. The same voice came back on, after five or six full rings.

"What?" he yelled with the machines still working in the phone.

"Hey! How the hell am I supposed to come down there and see your land if you don't give me the address?" I shouted. Grandma laughed out loud behind me.

The machine cut off. Silence. "No need to get sore about it, buddy. I just wanted to make sure you're coming," he said.

"Today? It's raining."

"Not here it ain't. You got a atlas?"

"I can get one in the car."

I heard him clear his throat. "Just get a ink pen and write this down. You can't miss."

"Hold on!" I smarted back. I saw through the phone a mountain man, bearded with beady eyes, rolling shoulders with a pot belly and legs spindly but whipcord strong, probably standing there in greasy jeans with oiled boots on his feet. "Grandma, you got an ink pen out there?" I asked, covering the phone. "This guy's getting on my nerves."

A wrinkled hand reached around the wall, a pen thrust in her fingers. "There you go."

I took the pen and made a few lines on the paper. "Okay, buddy, shoot."

"That's my name," he shouted.

"Buddy?"

"Buddy Ray. They just call me Buddy. Okay, so head down 77 all the way to 70 West. Take that into Zanesville and get off on 93 South. That'll go for a decent piece, ten mile, maybe." I scribbled away over the newsprint and repeated it. "Look for 13 South then. Take that all the way down to a town called Corning. You got it?"

"Thirteen south to Corning," I recited. "Got it. Okay."

"Okay, then. If you see signs for Burr Oak State Park, that

means you went too far. Turn around. But you can't miss Corning, trust me. So, coming down from the north into town, you'll hit Main—that's Route 155. The library's right there on the left side, a brick building. You'll want to go right there and just stay on 155 till you come to Scenic Road on the right."

"Whoa, slow down. Then Scenic on right. Okay."

"The sign's real faint so be looking. Hang a right there on the gravel road and go a piece up 'ere till you come to a fork. Scenic forks to the right, but you don't want that. Hook left instead on the road with no name. You can't miss it because you'll be looking dead on at two finger reservoirs. Now that unmarked road will take you right to the property. Down front along the road, you'll see our mailbox marked 'Bennett' with all gold letters. It'll be on the right."

"On the right, and it's 'Bennett.' Okay, I got it. How long a ride is it?"

"Should take you about two and a half hour, pert near three, from Akron."

I waved my hand, trying to gesture through the phone. "Okay, here's the thing. I got the cash at my house—enough to buy the place, and I'll need to swing by and get it. But it sounds like it's in the sticks.

"I'm wondering about jobs. See, the thing is, I got to be able to make a living down there. My girlfriend, too. She's a waitress and I'm into landscaping. Can we find work you think, in that Corning town?"

"Yeah, I suppose so," he said. "Corning's five, ten minutes from the house. Let's see, Bonnie's is down in Glouster. That's pretty good food. Then just past the turnoff a few minutes is the Shawnee Village. That's a restaurant over in Shawnee."

"That'd be good for her. She worked in a place before called the Village Inn. So, that's good, but what about me? I'd have to get something, too, for us to make a go of it."

"If you was to move down here, there's a plant right in Corning that might be putting guys on. If you're strong and can handle a chainsaw, hell, you might be able to come to work for me up at my place. I'd have to see you first. You ever do any lifting, hauling, that kind of thing?"

"Deadlifted five hundred pounds once, that should count for something," I said.

"That's not bad," he grunted. "You got possibilities down here. But you got to like the place first."

"That's right, I do. Well, Buddy, I guess I'll come down then. It's uh, let's see, almost eighty-thirty now, I'd say look for me somewhere around eleven-thirty. I got to get the money first. I'll be driving a big green Impala."

"What's your name, by the way?"

"Whitehall. Gary Whitehall."

* * *

How this day unfolded, from rainy city to country sun, from apartment living to country dealing, blew my mind. I fell in love with the endless acres of hardwoods, the little stream that trickled over stone beds running down the hillside, the cabin perched at the land's pinnacle. By the time I was coming back into Akron, I was fifty-eight thousand dollars lighter. Buddy had come down seven grand on the price after some dickering.

That's when I spilled my story to him—he seemed that honest. I told him everything—ATF, the investigation, Liz, being on the run, even trying to get rid of the money in the best way I knew how. He growled a great deal about the government, smiled when I told him how I had left it all behind and was on the run from the FBI and the bikers. The motorcycle gangs, he told me, "were animals in vests. They give real bikers a bad name."

And as far as someone being able to trace the money, he wrote the deed at $9,000 flat to keep me free of declaring my source. What money exchanged hands was between us, he said. His bearded jaw was resolute when he slammed his fist to the kitchen table. When we stood to shake on it, his hands were calloused and dry, his grip scary.

CHAPTER ELEVEN

I pulled into the apartment parking lot, raced up the stairwell and clicked open the door before I remembered Liz was at work. It was Friday night, her night to make a bundle. I showered and changed into new jeans and a collar shirt in minutes. I drew a scrap of paper from a drawer and scrawled a note in bold print, taping it to our locked door.

TIME TO CELEBRATE!

MEET ME AT THE BUCKET—

COME QUICK, THERE'S BIG NEWS.

(I'LL BE WAITING!)

I hoped she would have the energy to come over. It was Friday night, though, and the rain hadn't stopped. I burst through the door of the place and asked the smiling brunette behind the bar for a vodka and orange juice. I stood there, sipping the drink, fixed on catching a second rainy day off from work and a celebration with Liz that night. A permanent place all our own. Title and deed in hand. A place in the mountains with no strings behind us. The perfect life.

Then Robin came walking in.

Two steps behind her was a blonde girl with faraway eyes that scanned the place. I turned back to my drink when I heard Robin shout my name across the bar.

"Oh, hey," I said, feigning surprise, "how you doing?"

"Gary! What on earth are you doing here?"

"I live across the street," I said. "You know that."

"Well, either way, it's so great to see you," she gushed and threw her arms around my neck. Sickly sweet perfume, hairspray smell, familiar skin. She stepped back and cupped her friend's elbow. The girl's eyes stopped dancing around the place long enough to focus. "Gary, this is Katie. Katie, Gary."

The blonde extended a lithe arm toward me, her hand soft, an oversized diamond on her finger. She had straight, luxuriant hair that shone from endless brush strokes, great handfuls of it stopping at her cleavage. The silk dress she wore climbed up her tanned leg, stopping just short of indecent. She was wearing shoes with thin leather straps and chunky heels I knew Robin always went around in. Her makeup was heavy, and I guessed the beauty mark set on her cheek was a fake. "Pleasure," she said, "buy two girls a drink?"

"Uh, yeah," I said, "we can do that, I guess." I waved the barmaid over. "What do you have?" I asked, tipping my drink as they leaned in. Above the roar of the music, I heard Robin order a Cadillac margarita, her friend some other frou-frou drink. They turned to me and I smiled.

"So, where you from, Katie?"

"Canton." Her eyes had a silvery look to them, her lips tipped down at the corners.

"Ah. So, how do you know Robin?"

"We met at a party in the Valley. My boyfriend Mark works out with Derek," she said, nodding her head at Robin.

"Raff?"

"Uh huh," she said. I thought she rolled her eyes at me.

"So," I began, brushing past Robin and coming around to Katie's shoulder as drinks arrived. I tossed a twenty over their shoulders to the smiling barmaid. "I suppose you heard what a lousy guy I am from this one here."

Robin giggled. "Now, don't do that. We're just out having fun tonight, that's all."

Katie squinted at me and drained nearly half of whatever pink-colored booze was in the glass. I pictured her biting me or splashing the drink in my face. The orange vodka had already begun slipping through my arms, loosening them. Besides, the last person I wanted to see coming through the door right then was Liz, much less while I was hanging out with two prima-donnas. I opened my hand toward Robin. "Well, if you were willing to go over to my grandma's and lay a pack of lies on her about California, I can't imagine what you told Katie here."

"We're not out here for you," Katie cracked, rolling her lip and revealing perfect white teeth. They'd been whitened in a dentist's chair, I could tell.

"If that's the case, you can pay for your drink then," I said.

"Gary!" Robin shouted. "Stop it." She was inches from my face. Robin looked good made up and her eyes were still clear. She turned to Katie and made a strained smile. "Just give us a minute to talk, okay?"

"Whatever," the girl hummed, lifting her drink with two hands and moving toward the far end of the bar.

"Nice to meet you," I said, leaning toward my wife. "How many drinks today, Robin?"

She raised a hand of oath, resting her arm once more on my shoulder. "This is the first of the day," she swore, pointing her index finger at the cocktail. "I have a confession."

"Yeah, what's that?"

She whispered, "I thought about you since the time at Anna-belle's. A lot. I'll give it to you straight. I was just trying to get even, maybe break you and what's-her-name up." In the distance, an older tanned guy in a golf shirt had sidled up to Katie, who stood there, flailing her thin hands in expression.

"Are you serious?" I asked.

Robin's breath was against my neck, Carrie the barmaid gave us a strange look, and I pulled back from Robin's words. "I still love you, and I'd do anything to make it work. I'll even give this up, if it means getting you back and us staying together."

"Anything?" I asked. I needed her to agree to sign divorce papers. A black cloud of doubt perished the notion—*not here*.

Without warning, Robin leaned in and kissed me on the cheek. Her hands gripped me at the chest and neck as she nuzzled in my ear. "Let's go get a room somewhere," she murmured, flicking her tongue across my lobe, "and I'll get nasty for you, just like you want . . . like before. Remember?" She tipped her pretty head toward her friend, her eyes close to mine. "I can get rid of Katie, no problem."

I placed my hand at the small of Robin's back and pushed off from her. "I can't do that. I already got a girl."

"Pfft. Yeah, you got a girl alright." Her countenance changed to dull eyes that glanced at Katie's wave from across the bar, a second full drink sitting before her. We sat there side by side in silence, Robin and me, looking to the untrained eye as a couple with barstool blues. A thought crossed her face, and she snorted. "You know, your friend Stubbs had it in for you all along."

"I told you out there that he wasn't my friend. I hated that guy. Why, what'd he say about me?"

She laughed a hoarse, barfly sound. "What'd he say? He said you lied to them, that you lied to me, that you didn't care about me. Not anymore than the Man in the Moon. That's what he said, swear to God."

"I lied to them?"

She took a drink, a long generous gulp, and I pounded my hand at the bar. "That whole job was nothing but lies. Lie to the crook. Lie to the informant. Lie to this one. Lie to that one." The booze was clouding my memory from details.

"Informant," she scoffed. "Please, Gary. They knew all along you were banging that slut. That was all around your office. You just weren't smart enough to get it. So many people knew so much more than you thought they did. You fooled no one . . . ah, except yourself.

"That Stubbs guy said you were in denial. He told me that himself, said he and his wife felt sorry for me because you couldn't be trusted."

The place was filling up with groomed, raucous faces, most in their mid-to-late 20s, the thump of some industrial dance vibrating through the walls, growing louder with the increasing crowd.

A pair of women, both with poofy '80s hair and electric blue eye shadow, gyrated on top of the box seats along the wall. A crowd of men were clinking and raising long-necked bottles to them, and just then two hulking figures were opening the door. Because of the immense size of their necks and shoulders, they appeared to be swimming through the crowd with small heavy strokes. The beer drinkers all parted for them as they passed.

It was Raff. And following was a buddy of his with sculpted arms hanging from short sleeves, even though there was a chilly rain outside the door. From Katie's delighted squeal, her hero had arrived. I glanced toward the end where Katie stood flapping her wrist, delirious to show off to her chaperone down there. The guy in the golf shirt had a milky, wilted look on his face as he careened away from his barstool. Raff, in the meantime, had moved up behind us.

"Hey," I said, turning toward him, "what's up, man?"

"Gary," he said, tipping his head and gripping my hand where the knuckles folded together. His forearms were roped with veins. "Long time, no see, man." He smiled, his pearly teeth clenched. I reminded myself I should have been the angry one, and images of him lying nude on top of my wife blipped through my mind. *Sonofabitch.*

"You still up at Bodybuilders?" I asked. He nodded.

Robin pushed back from the bar, wheeled around and draped her hands to his chest, just as she'd done with me minutes before. "Can you hang out with Katie, hon, just for a drink or so?" she said, blinking. The effect was all hers. Raff grinned at her, his jaw striated. He rolled his shoulders, a cartoonish version of Mighty Mouse in a Metallica t-shirt. "Gary and I need to work out some things since he's back in town."

"You alright?" he asked her, his chest puffed and his back arched as he slipped his hands around her waist. The posture pissed me off, but I had difficulty feeling anything for Robin. I figured she posed in his arms to rile any jealousy she imagined I had in me. "I am fine," she said above the din. "Just need a little space, 'kay?"

He dropped his arms from her, lifting his chin toward Katie and her boyfriend Mark. Then he shouldered his way through the crowd in a slow, bowlegged gait. Robin resumed her seat, slapping me on the arm and leaving her hand at my wrist.

"So, tell me," she said, teetering a bit. The drink was a gulp away from gone. "You still in love with me or what?"

I shook her hand off me. "Quit it, Robin. I know what you're trying to do, trying to get this guy all fired up, so what—we get into it over you? Is that what you want? Two guys fighting over you?"

She cocked her head and pouted her lips. With a wave of her hand, she got the barmaid's attention as she pointed for another. "Well," she said, "it would be interesting to know you still cared."

"You screwing him or what?"

"Gary," she said and fawned. "Don't ask a girl that."

I smacked my lips at her. "I'm not. I'm asking you." Just then I caught a glimpse of Liz making her way through the bar, her work shirt still on, the moniker bow tie left cockeyed. I felt a rush of goodness seeing Liz.

"What's that supposed to mean?" I heard Robin cry in my ear.

"Oh," I announced, "here comes Liz. You be nice, I was just now." I faced Robin whose eyes burned a hateful glance through the crowd.

"The one coming over in a work shirt? What is she, a hostess or something?" Robin laughed, her lips parted in a smirk.

I glared at Robin. "Actually, she is. What's it to you?" I rose to greet Liz and when she came into my hug, I nestled against her and breathed a hello into her ear.

Liz stepped back. I studied her face for a response, though her eyes looked through me.

"I'm Robin, by the way." She pressed me aside and held out a hand.

Liz took it, shook it with a faint smile, and looked at me. She leaned toward me. "Is this the surprise? Meeting her?" Her voice had a slate quality.

"No," I answered, grinning. "I do have a surprise for you, though, later."

Robin's drink had arrived and Carrie, the grinning brunette, who continued dancing to the beat, leaned across the bar, her eyes fixed on Leslie's. "Getcha something?"

Liz pressed her fingers to the bar and leaned in. "Vodka tonic, please." The girl disappeared and from the corner of her mouth Liz mumbled what I thought was something about "making it a double." Her face reminded me of the time we'd sat in the parking lot at Smith's Bakery.

Robin's eyes, in the meantime, had been up and down Leslie's outfit. In a look of disdain, she turned back for her drink. "So, Gary, you might want to move past introductions here."

I held up my open hands at Robin, the universal *take it easy* gesture. I looked down toward Katie, who was studying us. Raff, too, looked confused over the three of us milling about the bar stools. And his buddy Mark, rocking back and forth, kept tapping his pecs and spitting in a chew cup.

I stood with my drink in hand as a fresh vodka drink arrived at my elbow. "You want a seat, honey?" Liz took the chair with a plopping movement. Robin stared at me. Liz, too. She lifted the glass and emptied half of it.

"I told Robin here that we moved in across the street," I offered.

"That's nice," Liz said.

"How was work tonight?" The words sounded garbled, like they were choking me. Robin's eyes danced with delight.

Liz nodded with lips pursed. "Great."

"Boy, are you on the hot seat," Robin laughed, jigging to the music and dipping her chin for another sip. "I love it."

My glass had been empty to ice cubes for some time, but no way in hell was I asking for another. I scowled at her. "Don't do that, Robin. We're going as soon as she has her drink."

"I came over because your note said to come quick," Liz said, with a wave at her clothes, her hair a strand or two out of place.

Robin looked at Liz, her eyes hard and flat. "So, you're the woman who breaks up marriages," she started.

"What'd you say?" Liz bared her teeth.

"You know, going around with him and your . . . heels up in the air," Robin continued, gesturing an open palm above her head.

"Whoa!" I said, stepping in. "Stop that."

"Yeah, and you're the woman who throws up everywhere," Liz said loudly over my shoulder.

Robin tore past my shoulder like I wasn't there, and I saw Raff on his way over. But Robin stood face-to-face with Liz, who remained on the stool. "Hey," Robin shouted, "I got one question for you. What's it like living with a murderer?"

"Calm down and I'll tell you," Liz sniffed, picking up her drink, though I could see her hand shaking. She sipped it and slapped her thigh with the other hand. "He's not a murderer. He's a killer, and there's a big difference."

"Oh, really?" Robin shot back. Raff was elbowing his way through.

"Uh huh," Liz hummed, "and I sleep like a baby next to him." She pointed her index finger in Robin's face as an introverted looking couple took a step back from us. "That is, when we are sleeping."

"Uh!" Robin squealed, "You know ATF told me all about you, meth girl. They said you're a biker slut and a wh—"

I grabbed Robin by the arm about the same time I felt Raff's hand on my shoulder. I leaned in to her. "You shut your fucking mouth, Robin!" I shook off Raff's hand, his friend barreling through the crowd behind him. "Back off, Raff!"

He lurched at me and I crashed from the force into Robin, who hit the wall behind me. As I pulled my arm with the drink free, I locked up with Raff, whose strength felt solid as stone. No way could I outwrestle him, his grip was a vice on my right shoulder. And I could see his friend charging at my free side.

Adrenaline coursed through me. I swung the glass in my hand as hard as I could at the back of Derek's head. Ice chunks and glass shards flew upward. The women against the bar screamed as Raff dropped to his knees, and his hand covered his neck. I saw blood. My hand ached from the glassy stump that remained in it, and seconds later the music stopped. Most eyes locked on Raff down on the floor.

Mark stepped back, his eyes wild with alarm. He threw up his hands awkwardly. Though my hand throbbed, it kept gripped the bloody glass. I wagged it at him. "You want some? Let's go!" I screamed above the din and a sudden circle of faces formed. In my mind's eye, I saw the old Western scene where someone had pulled a gun and no one knew what to do but stand there. I lurched toward Mark.

He threw open his hands at me. "Enough!" he roared, pointing at Raff on the floor. "He's hurt, man! Get the hell out of here!" I stood panting, looking around me. No one moved. Except Liz. She slipped behind and I heard the squeal of the door and more revelers arriving. A distant voice laughed from the street, "Aw, hell naw! We ain't going in there!"

The dancing barmaid was shaking her head, both hands resting on the counter. "I just called the police. You need to leave the bar, Gary. He's right," she yelled, nodding at Mark.

My hand burned with pain. "I didn't want any trouble. He grabbed me first—"

"Just get out of here!" the brunette screamed. "We don't want that shit in here." A few college boys roared and applauded the barmaid.

I felt small and sick. When I hit the door, I could see Liz running across Market Street in a drizzle, headlights reflecting the street against her black silhouette. The glass stayed clenched in my hand, and I looked back over my shoulder. But the door to the place never opened.

In the distance I could hear sirens shrieking. As I found my feet on the sidewalk across from the bar, I dropped the broken glass in the raised yard of an apartment building, wiping my ragged palm in the cool wet grass. Below me, I could see blood dripping to the walk, peppering it like dark coins. Behind me, I could hear a bluster of voices and a lone one shouting, "There he goes!"

When I banged into our front door with a shoulder, Liz jerked it open, her eyes wide with disbelief. And then she saw my hand. I stepped in, cupping the cut hand with the good one, a drip—drip—drip marking my path to the sink. I dropped my palm into the basin as she opened up the faucet. On the countertop I noticed my handwritten note from earlier.

"What the hell, Gary?" she cried. "What the hell?"

"Ah," I howled from the scorching pressure and agony compressed into the heel of my palm. "Not now, Liz. Ah, same damn hand as the one I cut in the cabin!"

She leaned in and took my hand. There was a sudden splash of light from her snapping the wall switch. "Let me . . . hmm. It's a gash alright," she breathed, "almost the same place as your other scar. You're going to need stitches for sure." She was beneath the counter, unraveling a roll of towels and wrapping a long band around and around my hand until it was bulbous and useless, a thin football made of absorbent paper. "Just hold that on it and I'll get some tape."

As she left the room and I wandered in to sit down on the couch, my body still trembling.

Someone pounded on the door and I rose. "Now what?"

"You Gary Whitehall?" A confident looking police officer demanded. Behind me, Liz stood with a tape dispenser at her fingers.

I hummed from my chest. "Yeah."

"Were you just now in an altercation at the Bucket Shop, sir?"

I nodded.

"Well, you're under arrest for assault."

Baffled, I stood there considering what had happened. "I don't get it. How'd you know where to—"

His eyes drew to the old runner that was spotted all the way down the hallway, curling in at the doorway where a smattering of drops had fallen. I sighed and someone was tugging at my hand. It was Liz with the tape. A second light-skinned cop clicked through the door down the hall, removing his cap as he strode toward us with a gasping two-way radio.

"Let me tape his hand, at least," Liz interjected. "Otherwise, it'll start bleeding again."

"You taking him in, then," the second cop asked. "'Cause I'm going back over to get a statement from the manager, and I'll just meet you down there at City. You cool?"

The first one grunted and, once the tape was around my hand, spun me around and jammed me against the wall. "Take it easy, man," I said, "I was one of you."

"Oh, yeah? Where at?" I felt the left cuff tighten at my wrist and it hurt, sent the palm throbbing again.

"Charleston area. South Carolina. Beach community out there," I said.

"Everybody's a cop or a lawyer when they're under arrest," he said, turning to Liz. "Your boyfriend got some ID?" She disappeared and I remembered our bundles of cash in the place, taped here, packed in there.

"Liz, my license is on the dresser," I called. I heard a door slam and footsteps coming.

"Here," she said. "Well, what do you want me to do?" I felt her hand at my shoulder.

The officer barked at her. "Ma'am, you'll need to step back and—Gary, is it?—I'll need you to spread your feet far apart." I walked my way to a wide squatting stance, my chest pressed against the wall. "Do you have any weapons or—"

"No weapons, no drugs," I barked over my shoulder. "I told you, I know the drill."

Liz closed the door of the place and stepped into the hall, her keys tinkling as I was being frisked. "So, what was the big surprise?"

"I can't get into that right now, honey. Honest."

"Sir, bring your feet back together for me," the officer said, "and we'll head out this way." I led him down the hall, his fist gripped around my elbow.

"Well, tell me it wasn't meeting your wife," Liz shouted. "Tell me that much."

I laughed. "Hell, no. Hey, and bring some money. I'm going to need bail."

I heard her locking the door. "I know what to do, Gary, all too well," she sighed.

"Ma'am, he might have to spend the night in lockup. I don't believe a magistrate's on duty to arraign him right now. You might want to wait till morning." He spun me once again and backed out of the building.

Liz marched toward us, her head down. "I'm coming!"

In the darkness, I saw the interior light of his cruiser as it idled. Sitting me in the back seat, he muttered in my ear, "You know, your friend across the street's got a pretty good sized gash on his head. Duty sergeant just might charge you with felonious, you know that?"

I waited for him to get in up front. The seats reeked of vinyl and puke, the air constrictive from the car's Plexiglas that separated us. "First off, he's not my friend, and did you get a look at the guy and his buddy? I was fighting two meatheads at once in there."

"What buddy?" he asked, dipping his chin at the handset. "Unit 10, dispatch."

A robotic voice clicked back. "Ten, go ahead."

He held up his hand to silence me. "Dispatch, I'll be en route to City Hospital at this time, one white male in custody, six foot, two hundred pounds, mid 20s, dark brown hair. He's going to need treatment for a laceration to his hand before booking, dispatch."

"Definite laceration," I mumbled.

"Copy, Ten."

"Ten out."

"Zero zero thirty-six hours."

CHAPTER TWELVE

The blue lights in City Hospital blared, and I walked in squinting with the officer at my hip. Once an admitting nurse had a chance to unravel Leslie's home bandage, my cut was demoted in medical priority. There'd been a gunshot wound that night that had taken a number of staff away from the ER. Plus, a boy swinging his arms all about for lack of breath was dragged in by some of my Appalachian brothers, all hog-eyed looking and undone in stained t-shirts and cutoff shorts, a real entourage straight from South Arlington.

I sat there holding my hand, nodding at Liz, who'd been asked to sit on the far side of the waiting room. When we had first arrived, Liz sat next to me and began quizzing me. "I got something to ask you," she said, glancing furtively at the policeman.

"Yeah."

"I went to look in my purse for my . . . a, my a . . .."

I looked hard at her and made a face at the cop on my other side. "Dwight Yoakam tapes?"

"Yeah. The tapes are missing. Did you know that?"

I nodded. "We'll talk later about it."

"What do you mean? What happened to my tapes, our tapes?"

The officer stretched and looked away, bored.

"I mean not now, that's what I mean. I'm going to jail and I don't want to talk about it now."

"But I want to know," she said. Her voice rose.

"Ma'am, I'm going to ask you to take a seat on the other side of the room. We're not going to have discussions right now," the blonde cop said.

Liz marched off in a huff and slumped down in a darkened part of the room. She forced her fingers into the stuffed chair and glared our way.

Just then Robin and Derek came wheeling out, Robin clinging to his arm with a sobered and tired looking face, medical papers clutched in her fingers. Derek hunched over with an ice pack on the back of his bandaged neck. She spotted me and stopped cold. "Real nice, Gary. Asshole."

An older woman with a boy whose head rested on her lap, his foot in a cast, looked up. The blonde officer next to me, whose name I'd come to learn was Fitz or Fitzy, stood up and raised his hands. He was about to say something when Raff pointed at me. "Your ass is grass, motherfucker. Hit me with a glass."

"Sir," Fitz began, "I'll ask you to leave this room at once. Otherwise you'll be joining him in the county jail tonight."

"You, too, bitch," Robin shouted. Liz shook her head.

Fitz strode toward her. "You're pushing your luck, lady," he said.

"Am I?" she challenged, her face defiant and puffy. "Maybe you should do your job and find out who you got in custody over there."

I glanced at Liz, who looked sick. Then back at Robin. The officer spoke up, "What do you mean by that?"

The air in the room was stifling. "I don't know," she said, wagging her finger at the cop, "why don't you ask ATF about Gary over there? Just see what they have to say about him."

"What are you saying, ma'am?"

She tilted her head my way, and I noticed her blouse had been torn at the sleeve. "Just ask the big fish," she spat. "We're out of here. Have a nice night." And the two of them limped through the big doors that hummed open.

"You have got to be kidding me," Liz said to the entire room.

Fitz turned back toward me. "Gary, how do you know her?"

I hesitated. "It's his wife," a voice answered.

The officer turned to Liz. "What was she talking about, 'ATF'? I thought he worked in Carolina."

"She's a drunk," I said, shaking my head. "You can't believe half of what she says."

Across the room, he demanded my license from Liz once more. The enormous wall clock I'd been watching for hours was now 3:15, the magical time I remembered being released from school each afternoon, a happy crossing of the clock's hands. The nurse called me back just then and I staggered through the unit, where the breezeway reeked of rubbing alcohol, and was told to lay back on a vinyl table covered in a broad band of paper.

"The doctor will be in soon to treat your hand," she said, sweeping the door to a popping close.

I felt shaky lying there, listening to myself breathe in the silent room. A couple fried eggs, maybe a sandwich of some kind, would have been nice. The doctor clattered through the door, his hair disheveled, his face and expressions decidedly Jewish. After several minutes of him rooting around in my palm to dislodge any foreign matter—great yelps of pain shooting up my arm at times—he began cleansing the wound and suturing the two flaps of meat back together. He worked without ceasing, bringing stitching thread from his sterile tool palette to my hand, little puffs of exertion coming from his nose.

With the hand bandaged and my person declared free to return to the officer in the waiting room, I stood on weary knees, slipped through the doors, rotating my hand to acclimate the nerves to their repaired state.

* * *

Liz sat weeping in the same chair where I'd left her. Her hands were slung behind her, the waitress top strange to the eye. I walked into the room, the old woman's boy now sitting up, alert to the scene. A voice erupted. "Gary Whitehall?"

Open-mouthed, I nodded at one of two men standing near the entranceway, both in blue jackets with FBI patches on their chests. He stepped forward and in a monotone voice announced to all present in the emergency ward, "You're under arrest."

"For what?" I laughed, an itchy feeling, almost clownish, bursting in my chest. For a flash second, I studied the door, the proximity of it to the men, the small chance of getting through it.

"You're being charged by the Federal Bureau of Investigation for the murders of Stanley Gorman and Ronnie Borrell. If you choose to make a statement, you may do so without counsel. Do you wish to have the benefit of counsel before we speak to you about the crimes you're being charged with?"

"Hell, yes, I want counsel. Definitely want counsel. That should be on record," I said just as loudly.

The agent, a Nordic looking man with broad shoulders and a rounded head that had gone bald before its time, winced and looked at Fitz.

"Are you taking custody here?" Fitz asked.

"What's going to happen to us, Gary?" Liz cried from across the room.

I dropped my head and shook it, tight-lipped. "Just don't say anything."

The second agent brought Liz to her feet and walked her over to our circle. The first agent with the loud voice began. "Okay, here's how this is going to happen. First off, we're transporting Gary and Liz to Hopkins Airport. Outside here, I'll call it in to the Marshals and see if they can have two of their guys on one of the early flights to Vegas."

"Vegas?" Liz sobbed. She looked sorrowful, her hair falling in strands. I remembered how the day had begun in Hocking County.

"Yes, Vegas," the agent repeated. "You're being extradited to Vegas to stand trial as the principal, I assume, for the killings. And you, ma'am, as his accessory."

"But we—" she said as I shook my head at her with pencil lips.

"Okay," he continued, "I'm Agent Gills, by the way. So, if you cooperate, you two will be on a plane this morning, on your way to Vegas courtesy of the United States Marshals Service. You'll be doing everything but gambling," he said with a false smile. His lips were unusually pink. He pointed a ball-point pen at us and clicked it. "You hungry?"

"I am, yeah," I said. Liz shook her head and looked at the floor.

"It's a three-hour flight, so you'll get a meal en route, and the Marshals from our Las Vegas office will be there to meet you at the airport when the Cleveland Marshals turn you over to them."

Fitz stood there listening, his radio crackling about a burglary that was underway on Arlington Street and Jonathan. "That's my old neighborhood," I said. Fitz smirked and turned down the radio.

"Officer Fitz," the lead agent continued, "I'll need your arrest report when it's finished, and please be specific on the circumstances of tonight—er, last night's—bar fight. That'll help the U.S. District Attorney's office in Nevada. Gary is being charged then by Akron, just so I know, with felonious assault?"

Fitz nodded and stretched into a yawn.

The agent unclipped a pair of handcuffs from his belt and moved toward me. I let my arms hang limp. "Mr. Whitehall, I'm going to cuff you now. Easy does it." A clicking lassoed my wrists in metal. "And Officer Fitz, is it? I'll forward a copy of our Transfer of Custody reports to your department when I get back from Cleveland. That guy he hit okay?"

"Doc said some stitches and a contusion at the base of his neck, but no concussion or anything. That guy just left here—big dude. He didn't seem real happy about our man here." Fitz winked at me.

Gills looked me up and down. "Hmm. Real bad guy, huh? You're not going to be an issue for us, I hope, on our little ride up to Cleveland?"

I rolled my eyes and shook my head. "No, I'm no convict."

The agent swaggered toward his partner with a tip of his head. "Hmm, note that in our transfer report. Spontaneous utterance."

Outside in the black Chevy Blazer, Liz rode in the front seat, her hands cuffed before her. If you had been driving northbound on I-77 in the predawn hours at the time, you might have looked over and saw Gills next to Liz and confused the pair for co-workers getting an early start on their workday. Behind her the younger agent rode next to me, the rear windows tinted solid black. I rode with my hands twisted behind me, Gills reaching speeds of 85 without blinking. "Defensive driving, huh?" I muttered, jiggling as we closed in on the steelyards of Cleveland and roared west toward the airport. My Adam's apple clotted my throat as I swallowed.

At the airport, a second pair of agents waited under a drizzly morning sky at an unmarked side entrance near the landing strip, the roar of planes screeching across the vast pavement. Within minutes, Liz and I were sitting on padded office chairs, slumped against the wall, nodding goodbye to Gills and his partner as the handcuffs were removed. I rubbed my wrists to soften the ache of the red bands left there. A larger man in khakis and a sports shirt, wire-rimmed glasses framing his face, stood before the two of us. He rotated the dial of his radio, calling somewhere in the airport for confirmation of our departure time.

"I'm Vince," he said, sitting on the edge of the desk. He looked confident in his hard mouth, catlike moves around the cramped office. I felt tired when I saw the freshness in this guy's eyes. "So, you were with ATF, Gary?"

"Yeah," I sighed, "that's right."

He opened a folder that had been laying on the desk under his thigh. "And it says here, that you, Liz, worked as a waitress." She nodded. "Hmm. Ties to organized crime. Huh. One meth charge, no other priors."

Liz rolled her eyes. "I'm not supposed to talk," she whispered.

Vince offered an open palm of assurance. "No, no, I wasn't trying to get a statement," he said, closing the folder, "just trying to get a feel for who we're flying with today, that's all. In fact, if you feel like talking about what's happened, I'd be the first one to suggest you speak with an attorney first. That's just me.

"As far as I'm concerned, we're just people flying from Ohio to Nevada, which, they say should be a good flight. It's light showers out there now, but we'll be fine by the time we get several thousand feet up."

I thought of Mr. Thrall just then, opening his landscaping shop and wondering where I was. Jimmy would be headed to Fairlawn alone today. Next to me, Liz scratched her chin and held my good hand, the first physical contact since our hug in the Bucket Shop.

"We're just waiting to get the call from the flight crew. See, we're going to board before the rest of the passengers, so we can get situated and comfortable. It almost always goes off without a hitch. Then, we'll strap in and get airborne and you'll be served a meal and—"

Liz shifted her feet and sniffed, "I am hungry."

"Good," Vince said.

I leaned against Liz. "It's going to be okay," I murmured with a squeeze of her hand, "we'll finally get to give our side of the story."

Vince frowned. He tapped my knee. "I see that you two are a couple and you want to assure her and all, but—" He stopped and pinched his lips between two fingers. "I'm going to ask that you two not communicate—just for now. Then, when you get to Las Vegas, you can say all you want. It's just that, for now, I'd rather not have to break out the paperwork and start making reports about any utterances. Gary, you of all people can understand that."

"I do."

"My flight partner will be here any second. And between here and the boarding gate, the four of us will walk the concourse real natural, no handcuffs—those are rules of the FAA. Besides, no need to panic the other passengers, right? We can't cuff you in flight, either. So, no funny stuff, okay?"

I nodded.

"Great, I can tell you guys'll be fine. And the thing is, Liz will be flying in the very front of the plane with Cheryl. She's real nice. She flies with all our female transports. Then, Gary, you and I will be all the way—"

The radio squawked and in the doorway stepped Cheryl, a light-skinned model of a woman with a razor-line haircut receding from her temple. "Time to move, folks," she said.

We rose at her entrance and set off for a brisk and lengthy walk. We were pointed to seats on the plane. Seconds later paying customers filled in around us. Vince lobbed a magazine into my lap as he sat across from me. "There you go, man," he quipped. "You an Indians fan?"

"Sort of." And other than what I wanted to drink in flight, those were the last words I spoke until we began our descent into the Nevada desert. Between the Salisbury steak and potatoes and the plane's humming locomotion, I dropped off to sleep in no time, the magazine curled over my thighs. I was awakened by a slap against my shoe's heel.

"Buckle up," Vince said.

The plane skidded and bounced, skidded and bounced, and taxied toward the gate. I heard seat belts clicking free. People around us hoisted themselves up, standing blankly in muggy compartment air, and through the fuselage, they all disappeared. A second set of Marshals met us at the cabin doorway to handcuff us before we'd even sniffed the desert air.

Within the hour, Liz and I stood before a magistrate with bushy eyebrows for our arraignment. Several factors of our case were established. We hadn't been given benefit of legal counsel. We were considered a "flight risk," which Liz called "ridiculous" under her breath. And the magistrate told us flatly that he was not a fan of ATF, that they too often crushed the rights of citizens and made his job that much harder. I stood silent.

I caught sight of a tanned, expressive man in the courtroom whom the Marshal identified as the lead agent in the case against us. The agent had an annoying habit of making a hissing noise between his teeth and working a toothpick between them. His jaw was unapologetic and he pushed and wheeled through the huddle of Marshals and court officers in the room. His name was Carbona, I was told. Francis Carbona. He peered several times around the much larger Marshals, glancing at us, his eyes watery. His mouth moved with the regularity of a piston. I caught a bailiff walking away from the group rolling his eyes.

"You and Miss Harlan will be separated until the trial," one Marshal said as he passed. "We're on our way with you to Clark County right now. You'll get to see the pre-trial officer over there. On your feet."

CHAPTER THIRTEEN

When the steel-plated door closed behind me and I studied the bunk suspended from the floor, nothing more than a human shelf built into cinder block, I sat down and wanted to cry. A dim fluorescent bulb flickered above the bed, and a stainless steel sink with push button service was but a foot from the jutting commode, no lid on the thing. The degrading sensation slowed me to blank staring. Orange sleeves hung from my arms, the jumpsuit thin at the knees. The cell smelled of offal. I kneaded my hands and sighed.

For several hours, I sat without much movement, twenty minutes without blinking. My breathing had slowed to a rate barely moving the cilia inside my lungs. I feared insanity was out there if this was to become my life. Even a year. Maybe a month. Could I make it? The hollowness expanded in my chest and I dragged my nails down the wall.

Could I maybe get some paper, a pen or pencil of some kind? They were officers like I once was, good guys joking between cell checks and prisoner movement. The difference glared at me; they were able to come and go as shifts turned. I sat here now, inside a man's guts. People whisked past outside the door's thick glass. No man, I reasoned, could break that glass.

I wanted to scream, but I didn't. That would be too much like prisoners I had ignored myself once I'd run them into county lockup. Uncuff. Print. Strip search. File paperwork. Schedule arraignment. Then get back in your cruiser and drive off. Job done.

The door clacked and swung open, its reverberation felt in my heels. A man in a dress shirt breezed in, planted his feet center floor, both hands wrapped around his briefcase handle, and tipped his head toward the door.

"Let's get you out of here," he said. "You don't belong in here." The deputy behind him whistled and wagged his keys, waiting. As we passed through the doorway, the man scoffed at the pre-trial paper in his hand, leaning in toward the deputy. "This one's too much, Jimmy. Guy's a veteran and a former ATF agent who blasted two meth dealers from Bakersfield. You'd think a parade, some statue in his honor? Oh no, that dipshit Carbona and his little buddy Aster throw this guy in jail. What a joke."

The deputy raised his shoulders and said, "What are you going to do? We don't judge 'em, we only lock 'em up." He slammed the door, leading us down the catwalk as the attorney roared on behind me. "Any counsel with half a wit would have a field day with this case. These dumbasses in federal courts, I swear. Talk about a waste of time and taxpayer dollars." I felt him nudge me from behind. "We're going down here to counsel rooms. Just follow our man up here. We'll shake when we get in there. Name's Riley, for the record, in case you're wondering."

We passed a Hispanic inmate sauntering toward his open cell, a trustee wearing a faded blue-green jumpsuit. Down the stairwell, the three of us followed a passage fresh with paint that led to a small meeting room. Inside, a table and three chairs around it symbolized its anxious space, a crushed flat coffee cup left for the next guy. I spread my legs over a chair and eased into it, folding my hands over the table as the deputy mumbled something to Riley.

"Before we go any further, what's your fee? I mean, I put down on the pre-trial papers that I wanted a good attorney, but I only have so much money," I said.

"Name's Vernon, but just call me Vern, okay? If you want my legal representation, Mr. Whitehall, we'll need a signed retainer. That's the law. And the fee for both of you—you and Leslie—will be fixed. I'll call it ten right now and we can sign papers," he said.

"Thousand?"

He blinked and pressed out his lower lip in agreement, his

hands moving over the papers before him. "I'd do it for free but I have a mortgage to pay over in Rancho Charleston and a Volvo installment that comes my way every month."

I shook my head. "That's too much, plain and simple. You know what the circumstances are. I got nothing to hide here. I mean, I don't want to go the court-appointed route with my freedom on the line—I've seen those guys. They're terrible. I could do a better job defending myself. But your price? Come on. Give me a break." I paused.

He fell silent, rubbing his brow, studying an empty part of the table. "I can go six and you'll not pay a penny more than that, and that's even with that assault charge last night mucking up your case. But I'll need three of it up front."

"Three thousand bucks, now?" I said, raising my voice. "You serious? How am I supposed to get that kind of money out here at the snap of a finger?"

He allowed his mouth to hang open, a watermelon pink to his tongue. "I don't care how you get it. Have someone wire it to you."

I started shaking my head. "Look, you're giving me a shakedown vibe on this right from the get-go. Work with me, hell. Otherwise, I tell the court I need another attorney. Seriously, I'm in a jam here, and I'm not bullshitting."

He raised his hand and tapped his knuckles against the table. I noticed his watch. I wasn't sure what a Rolex even looked like, but the gold band and intricate face on it wasn't purchased from a jewel case at Kmart. "Cards on the table, Gary. How much you got? Savings, stocks, retirement, whatever."

I thought about my remaining bundles strapped under two cupboard shelves at the apartment. I looked around the room. Sure enough, a camera was mounted in the corner. "I'm not saying anything with that thing on."

"It's off—look up there," he said, "see that dark glass bead? Well, when that's lit up, it's bright red. They can't violate our confidentiality by recording us in here. Hell, I wish they would. I'd have you walking out of this shithole this afternoon, know what I mean? You were law enforcement, you know the rules. Guys like me live for some dipshit deputy or cop to bend the law for a little glory and another collar." He leaned in, that mouth of his open again. He whispered, "That's why we have courts of law. So, let's stop wasting one another's time, huh? You confide in me, I defend you. Capiche?"

"You don't look Italian, Riley," I said with a smirk.

He threw up his hands. "You're a fed alright," he laughed, "another pain-in-the-ass stickler." I looked one last time at the lifeless camera. He was right. It was off.

"Alright, time to unload, huh? Okay, here's the deal. I give you seven grand in a cashier's check if you can get me out of this, and I'll sign any binding document you want to make that happen. That's a thousand more just for waiting for me to get back to Akron to mail it to you. And I do have cash. It's all in bundles in a certain place. And don't ask me where or how I got it."

He pressed his teeth to his lower lip and squeezed his pen. "I can draw that up. And it'll be balance due, one lump sum, within 30 days. That'll give you time enough to fly home, and shower and wash this place off your skin. But if I don't get my cashier's check, then I'll need to get nasty about this and hit you with a late fee. That's 20% for every month I don't receive it. How's that?"

"Yeah, okay."

"You'll sign it, and I'll give you a copy. In case you're wondering, that's another $1400 per month.

"And no partial payments, either. For example, let's say things get tight in your wallet, so you send me $6800 thinking it's your absolute best and close enough. Well, I'm still going to hit you with that $1400 penalty all the same. That's the deal on paper. It's fair. Take it or leave it." He extended a rather small hand across the table.

I shook it with vigor, recalling "The Devil and Tom Walker," the Irving story from high school English class, how the teacher kept telling us to watch who we make contracts with. And to walk away if it doesn't feel right.

"We'll get you and the girl out of here," he said confidently.

"Yeah, well, that Carbona guy scares me. Liz and I need someone with vinegar in his veins."

"Understood."

"So, now what, counselor?"

He turned to his brief, producing a legal pad for notes, and made a lengthy production of filling in our agreement for representation. He made guttural noises while filling it out as I looked around the room, standing and sticking my face into the unlit camera lens. He finished, slapping a hand on the table. "Okay! Don't get mad at me but this case screams for acquittal. And you know how?"

I shook my head, regaining a sense of relaxation. "Huh uh."

"You're a guy, Gary," he said, his voice cracking with rich appeal, "who quit his job. I mean, come on, you did what the rest of us dream about doing. All you did was walk away. You had your reasons, and you quit your job! Hell, they write songs about that."

I folded my arms and laughed. "Yeah, that tickles my ears, but what about the murder raps, Vern? I mean, two guys were killed up there in the desert for God's sake, and I was—" I looked up again at the camera. I dropped my voice to a husky whisper, "I was the one who pulled the trigger."

"Self-defense," he said, "even the FBI report alludes to the notion that those two animals were busting caps into that little cabin from the outside. Now you tell me. Am I right?"

"You're damn right," I said with a bump of my fist against the table.

"You want a soft drink?" he asked out of the blue. I made an agreeable face. He reached back, cracked open the door, and hollered like a farmer in the fields. "Hey! Jimmy!"

I heard the pounding of feet and, as they came closer, the tinkle of keys. "What'd you need, Vern?" a voice outside the door asked.

"Can we get a Coke in here for our defendant?"

"Sure, Vern. Give me a minute, okay?"

Vern grinned. "Great, Jimmy," he said, smiling all over himself. "You know this guy's one of you?"

The voice came again. "Yeah, it's all around the observation deck. Guy's a former ATF agent." Hairs on the back of my neck stood up.

"Right, Jimmy," Vern said, hanging his mouth open again, "so let's treat him right, huh?" The door closed again. Vern leaned back into the desk, beaming. "They love me here, these guys do." He raised his tiny index finger. "That's because, unlike some of these other Ivy League pricks around town, I treat these guys as my equal. And they always give me gravy treatment when they can."

He raised an open palm to his face and whispered, "Plus, don't say anything, but I got the sergeant who works afternoon shift off the hook after he got pinched out in Henderson for drunk driving. He was leaving an F.O.P. bash out there. Poor guy had four beers and a shot of Hennigan's and some rookie kid pulls him over, figures he'd make a name for himself by running in Sarge, you know?

"Sarge was lucky in that one. Because I had that kid second guessing himself and babbling on the stand when the justice ruled to dismiss." He leaned back in his chair, waving a hand at it all. "And when they threw a party to celebrate it, they invited me as a special guest. Phew! Now, that was a night of drinking."

"And you didn't get pulled over yourself going home?"

He shook his head with a smile. The door cracked open and Jimmy appeared with two cold cans of Coke, handing them down to Vern. I looked up at him and he caught my eyes and studied me. I tipped my head at him as he turned to leave. I leaned over, cracked open a can, and sipped with a burp trailer. "Thanks. What, these guys pay for your Cokes?"

"Nah," he said, "I pay on account every so often. So when I want something—cigarettes, a soft drink, candy bar—they'll get it from the commissary and bring it, if the right guy's working. Naturally, there's a jerk or two in here."

"Always is," I said.

He dove back into his briefcase, producing a formal looking report. "Now, back to the fun stuff. This little gem comes from ATF, your boss there?"

"Yeah," I said, piqued by the official document with our seal on it, "Brad. Guy's name is Brad Wilson. He's a good guy."

Riley snorted and ran his fingers through thinning hair. "Well. Okay, see, here's the thing. He may have been a good guy to you in the office, as you were working there, but somebody in ATF—whether in your office or headquarters or what—has a hard-on for you. And after having read this, I'm guessing it's about saving face. You embarrassed their bureau, you know, showed them up. That whole deal with abandoning your G-car outside the Bakersfield PD headquarters? You made them look bad, Gary, and now they're on a witch hunt."

"Okay, so what about it? They trump up a charge on me to get even? I mean, what all's in that report, anyhow? Do I get to read it?"

He slid it across the desk. "Go ahead, check it out. When you're done, I'll ask some questions, and we'll get set for a pre-trial hearing. Are you averse to a plea bargain?"

I rested my forehead at the side of my hands. Scanning the narrative, I glanced up at him. "Depends on what they offer." The paper looked official and when I saw Brad's name at the heading, I felt assured.

TO: J. Blatch, Special Agent in Charge, ATF, San Francisco, CA
FROM: B. Wilson, Resident Agent in Charge, ATF, Fresno, CA
DATE: 25 May 1990
RE: Resignation of ATF Agent Gary Whitehall

This communication is intended to serve as a preliminary report on the termination of ATF Agent Gary Whitehall, Fresno field office. Agent Whitehall was hired in the Fresno, CA field office on 23 Sept 1989. Pursuant to his hire, Whitehall successfully completed his assigned training, Criminal Investigator School (CIS). Among other tasks and duties Whitehall was assigned, he served initially as the lead agent in the investigation of Stanley Gorman of Bakersfield, CA. Gorman is a known narcotics trafficker and felon, who was believed to possess firearms, a violation of Title 18.

During the course of his investigation, Whitehall revealed to this writer and other agents in the Fresno office that he had come into contact with a confidential informant, Leslie "Liz" Harlan of Bakersfield. In that same period of time, Whitehall discovered that Harlan was the live-in girlfriend of the suspect under investigation, Stanley Gorman. A short time later Agent Whitehall revealed to his superiors that his relationship with Harlan had compromised the ATF code of conduct with respect to handling confidential informants (see attached statement, Stubbs).

Subsequently, the Stanley Gorman investigation was reassigned to ATF Agent Keith Stubbs. It should be noted that ATF Agent Whitehall was counseled by his training agent and this writer on multiple occasions regarding appropriate agent conduct with respect to informant Harlan. Despite being reassigned to a different case for investigation, Whitehall continued personal contact with Harlan without authorization. For the record, Whitehall denied any sexual relations with Harlan. Harlan has a criminal record for possession of a controlled substance, methamphetamine. When Agent Stubbs confronted Whitehall on the breach of conduct and mentioned possible disciplinary action in accordance with bureau regulations, Whitehall responded inappropriately and an argument ensued, in which Whitehall made a veiled threat to assault Agent Stubbs (see attached statement, Stubbs, 2).

On 17 May 1990 ATF Agent Keith Stubbs led a team of agents and local law enforcement officials in the service of a search warrant at the residence of Stanley Gorman (#90-1514 M). Agent Gary Whitehall participated in the raid. Though Gorman was not present, he did appear later in the day and was summarily taken into custody by a team of ATF agents—Agents Whitehall, Stubbs, and this writer. During his arrest, Gorman inquired into the whereabouts of his live-in girlfriend, Leslie Harlan. When Stubbs denied having knowledge of Harlan's location, Gorman insinuated that ATF Agent Whitehall knew of her whereabouts and was concealing information from all parties. It is noted that Agent Whitehall strongly denied having such knowledge and threatened to assault Stanley Gorman while the defendant was in handcuffs (see attached statement, Stubbs, 3).

I squinted at the document. "What a statement this is: 'counseled by his training agent'. Pfft. More like 'hassled'. 'Made veiled threat to assault'? Come on, Brad," I whispered. "Guy was talking about my wife there. This damn thing makes it sound like I was ready to blow while the training agent did nothing but provide gentle counsel." I lifted my eyes at Vern. "You believe this shit?"

He shrugged. "Somebody will. He's a decorated agent. Look for facts that are disputable, okay? Something to discredit in court, something we can prove is false. That's what we want, not whether you got along with somebody or not. Get the picture?"

I scanned another page.

On 21 May 1990, the Fresno ATF office received telephone communication from Detective James Moorehead, Narcotics Division, Bakersfield Police Department. The detective reported receiving a telephone call at approximately 1122 hours. The male caller identified himself as ATF Agent Gary Whitehall and requested that Moorehead notify the Fresno ATF office on his behalf. According to Detective Moorehead, Whitehall said he was leaving employment with ATF and that his government vehicle was parked in front of Bakersfield Police Department headquarters along with a letter of resignation of his position, addressed to ATF Fresno.

When asked about the whereabouts of Leslie Harlan, Whitehall admitted to Moorehead, "She's with me now." Whitehall requested that Moorehead cancel the missing persons report on Harlan, previously filed by Stanley Gorman (Kern Co. M.P.R. #23777). Moorehead advised Agent Whitehall that he would have to speak with Harlan personally in order for him to cancel the bulletin. A female identifying herself as Leslie Harlan came to the phone and made statements to Detective Moorehead that identified her as Leslie Harlan of Bakersfield. Harlan stated that she was safe and that she wanted no further contact with Stanley Gorman (see attached statement, Moorehead). Detective Moorehead also warned Harlan and Whitehall that Stanley Gorman had posted bail that morning and was out of jail at that time.

Following the call, Moorehead made an immediate check of the Truxton Street side of the building, resulting in Bakersfield PD recovering a 1977 green Oldsmobile sedan matching the description of the vehicle issued to Agent Gary Whitehall. A note affixed to the windshield wiper read "PLEASE TOW THIS VEHICLE TO ATF FRESNO". As a precaution, the Bakersfield PD bomb squad opened the vehicle, without incident (see attached statement, Moorehead 2). Recovered inside the vehicle's trunk was government-issued equipment, including but not limited to the following items: ATF jacket, protective vest, credential with badge, charge cards (2), handcuffs, flashlight. Also surrendered were a shovel and bolt cutters, though neither item was issued by the Fresno ATF field office. Agent Stubbs and Agent Christopherson of this office were dispatched to Bakersfield to retrieve the vehicle and equipment (see attached ATF Inventory).

Also found in the vehicle was correspondence addressed to this writer at the Fresno ATF office. Inside a business envelope was a signed letter of resignation from Gary Whitehall. The signature in the letter matches handwriting exemplars of Whitehall. The resignation letter was tendered by Whitehall via the Bakersfield Police Department (see attached exemplar, Whitehall; letter dated 21 May 1990, Whitehall).

On 23 May 1990 this writer received a telephone call at 0016 hours from the Inyo Sheriff's Department of Independence, CA. Lieutenant Garland Miller reported to this writer that on 22 May

1990 at 2137, his department received a complaint for shots fired at a mountain cabin in the area of Lower Haiwee Reservoir. Inyo County Sheriff's Deputy Anthony Pinelli was dispatched to the area, where the complainant indicated to Pinelli the location of gunfire, the vacation home of Brian and Rochelle Williams of Las Vegas, NV. The cabin and property owned by the Williams' is located at 6122 Highway 395, Lone Pine, CA.

Upon arriving, Pinelli discovered two male victims outside the cabin, both apparently deceased as a result of gunshot wounds. Ridgecrest General Hospital paramedics were called and arrived on the scene a short time later. EMT Shane Buford examined the bodies later determined to be Stanley Gorman and Ronald Borrell. Buford found no vital signs in either body. Gorman was pronounced dead on the scene at 1051 hours on 22 May 1990 as a result of multiple gunshot wounds to the chest and head.

On 22 May 1990 at 1055 hours, Ronald Borrell was also pronounced dead on the scene, due to bleeding caused by a single gunshot wound to the upper thorax. (See attached, Ridgecrest Hospital reports #900522BOR, #900522GOR).

A check of a suspicious vehicle parked along Highway 395 traced the automobile back to Roger Borrell, 1201 Mount Vernon Avenue, Bakersfield, California. Kern County deputies were dispatched to Borrell's residence. Borrell stated to deputies that he had loaned the car to his son, Ronald Borrell of Bakersfield. Ronald Borrell allegedly told his father he and his friend Stan Gorman, also of Bakersfield, were going to the mountains that day for a hunting trip. The senior Borrell's description of his son matched that of one of the victims at the shooting. Pinelli found no identification on either victim but did discover a plastic bag containing a small amount of an unknown white crystalline substance on the body of the second victim believed to be methamphetamine.

He contacted via telephone the Kern County narcotics division, where he spoke with detective J.W. Robbins for information on Borrell and Gorman. Robbins described Stanley Gorman over the telephone. Again, the physical description matched the deceased on the scene for Deputy Pinelli. Detective Robbins recommended that Pinelli contact ATF, explaining that Gorman had been recently arrested and charged with manufacturing methamphetamine, along with a number of federal gun charges (see attached statement, Pinelli).

Initial homicide reports issued by Inyo County SD indicate a gun battle at the above residence on the night in question. Two Colt .45 pistols, serial numbers #331298 and #711406, were found on the scene, both registered to Ronald Borrell. A 20-gauge single-shot Harrington and Richardson shotgun (serial #AL287502) was located inside the cabin, along with a partially full box of Foster rifled slugs. When news of the double murder broke in the local community of Bishop, a sporting goods merchant came forward the following day. Charles Prodenawicz of Mac's Sporting Goods produced a bill of sale dated 18 May 1990 for a shotgun matching the serial numbers found on the firearm recovered at the scene. The customer of record shows Gary Whitehall, 15750 North Biola Avenue NE, Fresno, California. (See attached Inyo County Sheriff's Department Incident Report #90-4509; also see Inyo County Employee Statement, Pinelli).

No other persons were found at the cabin. Following his phone conversation with Detective Moorehead of Bakersfield PD, Gary Whitehall has had no further contact with law enforcement. Likewise, Leslie "Liz" Harlan is believed to have absconded as Whitehall's accomplice. Both Whitehall and Harlan are at large as of the writing of this report. No criminal charges have been filed by Inyo County Sheriff's Department as of this date. Given the volatile nature of the circumstances surrounding this case, the

Federal Bureau of Investigation, Las Vegas office, is conducting an investigation into the deaths of Stanley Gorman and Ronald "Ronny" Borrell.

"Okay, this part's true. But that bit about me threatening to assault Gorman while in handcuffs? No way. I'd never hit a guy in handcuffs, never. In fact, I once stood up for a prisoner when I worked with this Southern cop who used to slap drunks around that he'd drag in from the beach."

"Can you prove that?"

"If I have to, but how? I mean, that's been years. That guy's been fired since then, and I don't know if any of the others would even remember that. There was one dude who hated the guy. He might testify, but I hear he's in the Narcotics Squad in Charleston now. Why's he going to fly out here for this?"

He was scratching away on his pad. "You never know, let's leave it open."

I read on. "Okay, so I turned in my equipment and my letter of resignation was tendered. That was good. But these owners of the cabin, I wonder if they got the two thousand in cash Liz and I left behind. It doesn't say here—"

The pencil stopped. "You what?" Vern asked.

"We left behind right on the counter, two thousand dollars in an envelope and even marked it for the owners, so they could see we were sorry for breaking in and staying there without permission. For the broken door and all the gunshot holes left in the siding. There was glass everywhere. I just wonder what the bill was." I sniffed and rubbed my nose.

Vern's glasses were folded in his hand, one end dipped in that open mouth of his. "Would you swear to that in court?"

I nodded. "Yeah. It's the truth."

"Oh, this is good. This is really good. Nowhere in Wilson's report does he even make remote mention of this. And then there's Inyo County. I won't disparage any of the boys in blue, but what happened to the cash for restitution? That act alone shows a spirit of remorse on your behalf. Without its mention, the document looks like you broke into a guy's vacation home, trashed it, and left it all shot to bits.

"Someone's going to need to answer for that. I mean, this kind of thing is all part of the evidence chain. It should be front and center, but your boss chose to leave that detail out. And it's very consistent with the way you left your car, the penning of that letter. It's all very conscientious, Gary, and it all bodes well for you and Liz." He slipped into his glasses, nodding at the report.

I slurped at the Coke and burped again. "Sorry. So, they had meth on 'em. Hmm, I guess Liz was right. Stan was on the drug when he came walking into gunfire, like a zombie. He just kept saying he wanted his girl back."

"Oh, tell me he wasn't unarmed when you shot him, tell me that much."

I tipped my head for details. "Um, you know, I forget. The whole deal went down so fast—"

"Think, Gary. Think. No way can I put you on the stand as a witness if you can't remember that very key detail. Well, they can't either, for that matter. But, man, you've got to think he was blasting when you were blasting and you just happened to get the better of him."

"Wait a minute," I said, "you need to write down in your note-pad that these guys both had semi-automatic pistols. I was fighting back with that damn youth gun they mention in there. A puny little 20-gauge single shot that guys hunt doves and small game with. I mean, I did have the rifled slug, but Vern, I was so outgunned from inside that cabin, I thought we were both dead. Put that down."

"Twenty . . . gauge . . . small game . . . outgunned by auto pistols, got it. Now, before we finish the report, why'd you do it?"

"Do what?"

"Why'd you kill these guys?"

I scratched my head. "Vern, they were coming up to an isolated cabin to kill us. They were both armed with pistols. I was with a woman, his woman. If she hadn't suggested it, I wouldn't even have bought that shotgun."

He scribbled more and more, pausing. "Interesting," he said. "Any other reasons for pulling the trigger?"

"Yeah, one good one. That guy used to beat her—Liz. The poor girl was living in fear, especially after he'd come back from a cook in the desert. Look, we both wanted out. It's as simple as that."

"Oh, that's good, that's so good," he said. I went back to the report.

Since Whitehall's resignation predates his alleged actions in Inyo County, ATF may be exonerated from the murders that took place. Former Agent Whitehall was out of the purview of his previously assigned duties. This writer recommends all retroactive pay and benefits due Gary Whitehall and his wife of record be canceled. Mrs. Robin Whitehall stated via telephone on 24 May 1990 that she is currently estranged from her husband, she wishes no further contact with him, and has since relocated to Akron, Ohio.

"Okay, so they know where I got the gun . . . which I left. And so on and so on. So, I see here, they canceled any salary. Geez. They tried to extricate themselves from what happened.

"Eh, what am I going to do? And what's this here about my wife, Robin? Oh, that's rich. 'Wishes no further contact with me'? That's why she offered to sleep with me just last night in a bar. No further contact. Yeah, right."

Vern, for the first time in our counselling session, looked uncomfortable.

"Hey, man, don't look at me. She's one of the reasons I got the hell out of California. It's hard to say it, but she's a damned drunk. And for the record, which you'll soon discover, she's the big mouth that got me on a plane out here. I hit her boyfriend with a cocktail glass last night—that's another long story."

"Tell it," Vern said. And on we went, wrapping up hours later, once I'd answered questions about the cabin, the cash (which he decided did not exist), our escape that night to the casino, the stint in Flagstaff, and everything that had happened in Ohio since our return. My mouth was dry. There'd be more meetings, he promised, over the next few days.

And I went back to that horrible cell, stretched out on the bed, and slept for hours.

CHAPTER FOURTEEN

For three days I did not see my attorney, taking hard workouts with Olympic weights when they were available in the mornings, writing on scraps of paper during my cell time, and avoiding conversations with other inmates for the most part. When Jimmy came by to talk one night, he told me most guards knew my case from the newspaper, that it was big news, that even a few inmates had caught on. I would be monitored for chance reprisals among the general population. Two bikers were awaiting sentencing for assault on a grocer, he explained, though they were from a Vegas gang.

On the fourth day, the door swung open, and in marched Riley. I sat upright, rubbing my thighs and ready to talk. He shook his head and waved his hand. "Ah! Hold it. This'll be quick. I have to be at an arraignment, a federal hearing. But here's what I have," he said, sitting next to me on the bed and rifling through his attaché, slipping free a manila folder. "Aster has sent me a list of witnesses, but more importantly, an offer for a plea deal. You interested?"

"What's he offering?"

Riley pursed his lips. "Well," he said and hesitated, "it's like this: they'll drop the murder charges in exchange for guilty pleas to the charges of obstruction of justice and neglect of duty. You'll get one year but with good behavior, be out of here and on your way back home to Ohio in six months. Now, considering everything, I call that a good deal. Hell, I'll even cut your fees in half. You'll owe me $3500." He rolled his wrist over and snapped his arm to full extension, reading his watch. "I can squeeze this in, we can sign papers on their offer right now if you want, down in the meeting room. It's up to you."

I shook my head and mumbled, "I don't know, Vern. Six months in a prison cell?"

"It's a federal pen, Whitehall. They're hotels these days. Minimum supervision. Guys come and go, it's a country club for cripes sake." His eyes bulged with excitement.

I flopped my hands to my lap and sat back. "No, no way. I'm not telling them I'm guilty. 'Cause I'm not. I quit my job. I defended myself and Liz. That's all. You said it yourself, Vern. What happened to that?"

He blew air through his lips. "It might get a little more complicated than that if we take this thing to trial. And that sonofabitch Myer Aster. He'd throw his own mom in prison if he could. I'm just telling you, swallow hard, because this guy is going to bring up every speck of dirt on you that he can scrape up." He waved the file and started to open it but then closed it. I felt nervous, a little sick. The charisma I'd seen was missing from his face.

"What?"

"For one, he intends to put Liz on the stand."

"To testify against me? Can he do that?" My voice rose an octave, feminine and shaky.

"Hell yes, he can do that. He's the US Prosecutor, and he's got it in for you. I sat in with him and Liz, and Aster offered her the moon. Complete immunity from criminal liability. All in exchange for her testimony. And that prior of hers for meth? He waved that around as a scare tactic."

I cocked my head, hurting in the center of my chest. "She said she would testify against me?"

"No choice," he said, "you two aren't married. He can force her to testify, and unless she's completely cooperative, he can charge her with what you're looking at. Face it, you two are the only witnesses to what happened over there in Lone Pine. He even said to her with those damn little beady eyes of his, 'we don't want you, Liz. It's Gary we want.'

"See, that's what I told you. These are men working for the same employer you took a hike from. They're all feds and they've got it in for you, man."

"Lord," I whispered. I swallowed and slouched back against the wall. "Six months."

"However, I still think they have no case," he said, slapping me on the knee, "so let's not write our epitaph just yet. Trust me, I know Aster. If he had you in the cross hairs right now, there'd be no need for Liz, and there sure as hell wouldn't be any plea deal coming out of his office. He knows his case is shaky, and if you want to stand on what we have, more power to you. I'll give it everything I've got to see you walk."

I took a deep breath and began pacing in the cell, Vern sitting there in silence. "I don't know, Vern. I just don't know. I mean, can I think about it at least?"

"Sure. But remember, this is a chess match, and if we put up an uncertain front, that just builds up that asshole. Off the record, I'd be ashamed if I were Myer, putting one of his own on the stand, and all for taking out two of society's worst. I tell you, it's not about that. This case is about saving face, sending a message to any other would-be maverick agents out there. You don't screw around with the principals in an investigation. I can guarantee you Washington is watching."

I leaned against the wall, rolling my eyes. "Maverick," I repeated.

Riley shifted on the bed and held up a blank legal pad. "Gift. This is for you. I want you to make notes on it, write down anything you might think is relevant to proving your innocence. This will help me prepare for your case, if that's the route we're going to take. Obviously, you'll take the Fifth, no need to throw you up there in front of Aster.

"Now, sit down here for a second. I want you to see the list of witnesses he's subpoenaed to testify."

I sat next to him and began scanning the page. "Well, let's see. There's the guy from the Bishop gun shop. And Stubbs. I look for him to show up hostile. He was always threatening me with disciplinary write-ups." I stabbed at the printout with my index finger. "But what's with the clerk from Bally's?"

"I'm not sure, Aster doesn't have to disclose the nature of his testimony. Tell me, did you reveal something to this guy?"

"No."

He nodded, "Okay, well, think about it, try to remember what happened at the check-in desk. And who's that William Williams of Bakersfield?"

I threw up my hands. "William Williams? No clue . . . wait a minute. That can't be. Aw, are you kidding me? He's bringing in Billy Williams from the Red Hawks? Seriously? The guy's a biker.

"Liz's brother claims he's taken over as president now that Stanley's gone. And, by the way, they beat the crap out of her brother just for knowing us. And he's going to testify against me? For what?" It struck me. "Ah, the money."

"The hundred grand?" he asked.

"Yeah, I know that's got to be it. Can they charge us, Vern, with taking meth money? We wanted to do nothing but good with that cash, you know, turn it into something good instead of more chemicals for the street."

Riley pinched at his lip. "Hmm. Tell you what. Let's just deny it for now. Deny you know anything about it. You never saw it, you don't know anything about some wild cash claim. Didn't you tell me they had buried it? They buried meth money. Tell me that's not an admission of black market activity. None of those guys look like they lived through the Depression, you know, when working people distrusted the banks and were prone to bury cash. I say let their side raise the issue and I'll sink that ship gladly."

"But a denial? That's lying, Vern. I don't want to lie anymore. I promised Liz." I was on my feet, anxious.

Riley stood up, the top of his head did not clear my chin. His face turned baby-bottom pink. I bit my lip not to grin as he raised his finger at me. "You want to go prison, Gary? Huh?

"Now, listen to me, damn it. You can't go into this thing all cavalier and spouting a bunch of bullshit ideals. Couch that crap. You're facing a murder rap for God's sake, and this guy's offering you six months!"

I shook my head. "I get what you're saying. But for the record, tell the U.S. prosecutor I said 'no deal.' And I'm sticking to it."

Riley slouched and turned to his legal pad with a snort. "Okay, give me your suit sizes. We're going to trial."

* * *

Buttoning up a dress shirt and fitting a crisp neck tie with a knot felt strange the morning of our trial. Six and a half weeks had passed. The slacks and suit jacket fit my arms and chest without a sag—Riley had good taste. "Part of your bill," he said, dropping them off with specific instructions for a jailhouse haircut and perfect shave. Even the colors, he swore, mattered. My tie was pale yellow, the dress shirt powder blue, and a dress suit right off the rack at Penney's. I was going in navy blue.

Jimmy opened the door. "Damn, Whitehall, you look good today. In fact, some of the fellows might want some alone time with you," he joked. "Let's get you escorted to federal court. It's just a few blocks away."

"That's a good one, Jimmy," I said as he snapped on a pair of cuffs up front and we cut through the catwalks, "and now it's time for me to go over here and clear my name, get this shit off my back, know what I mean?"

He jingled the keys. "Yeah. We'll take those off when we get there. Marshals will be waiting. You got your notebook and your pen. Look like a damned attorney, man. Straight up." Down the steps and up into the van we went. Jimmy hoisted himself behind the wheel and slipped into mirrored glasses. It was sunny out. "Fellas all pulling for you, Whitehall. All but Mead. He says he don't like you."

"Well," I sighed and stared at the passing buildings, bracing my feet to the shifting lanes of the van, "Mead's an asshole. I think we all know that."

Jimmy burst out laughing. "I'm not saying anything."

At the rear doorways, a heavyset black man in a court blazer greeted Jimmy, looking past me until the county cuffs were off. Then he stepped up and jostled me, gripping the back of my arm with an unnecessary show of strength. "Come on, ATF," he harrumphed, jerking me forward through the hall, "and there damn well better not be any jackassing up here in my courtroom, you feel me?" He came close and his breath was stale, oniony.

I stared ahead and thought of guys like him: Stubbs, Mead, the guy from Carolina who hit prisoners. Jimmy's words of encouragement were ringing in my ears so I didn't care. Once he escorted me to the front table where Riley sat mulling over reports, the Marshal retreated to the back of the room.

I'd walked right past Liz without paying her undue attention, under the advice of Vern, who had told us that conservative jurors would frown on our relationship, no matter how jaded my marriage had been. Though we'd exchanged letters between jails, our correspondences had been limited to expressions of encouragement and hope, each mailed without a stroke dedicated to the circumstances of our case. I stole another glance and caught her eye. She flashed a smile and turned away.

She looked stoic, sitting just two rows from the front. The soft vanilla blouse she had on was buttoned up almost to her neck, and when I had passed, I saw on her feet a pair of flat heels of the same color and a modest khaki skirt far below her knees. Breaking her make-up routine, she wore faint pink blush on her cheeks and light eye shadow. I wanted to call to her and compliment her earrings, small gold beads. But I sat there with my back to her.

"Good morning, sir," Riley said, looking up.

"Mr. Riley," I replied. "We ready?"

"As we'll ever be," he said, "and the suit looks good. Well done."

Within a quarter hour, the jury had filed in, a bailiff had taken his place near the bench, and a mouse-like woman hunched over her stenotype, looking over her fingernails in the meantime. Behind me, I was alarmed to look past Liz and see three men in biker jackets stretched over the back row. One elbowed the other, and all three glared back.

"Are those Red Hawks back there?" I asked, my stomach knotting to a quick fist.

Riley turned his tiny head and peered over the top of his eyeglasses. "Appears to be." He whirled back around and sat mesmerized with various documents. "They've the right to be here just like any other citizen."

"Citizen," I whispered. A small bead of sweat rose on my lip and I lifted a plastic cup of ice water before me and quenched my dry mouth with a faint shake to my hand. "They make me sick," I choked. I plopped out the legal pad before me and ran circles at the top of the page until the ink ran from my pen. I tapped my fingers. It was after nine.

"All rise!" the bailiff shouted, his voice bassy and indifferent. A door adjacent to him swung open and a middle-aged woman entered, wearing a loose-curl permanent and a black robe. The bailiff recognized her by title and name and up the steps she went. She exchanged cordialities with Riley and then Aster across the aisle. As we all sat, I studied the prosecutor and thought of Riley's caricature. He was right. The guy was a human rat without the whiskers. I caught his eyes at one point, stopped on me.

The magistrate's name, the case number, the case, even my name—all announced without me hearing them. Until opening remarks were made, my stomach stayed knotted, my brain failing to process what was being set down as public record. I was numb until I heard the silvery voice of Myer Aster.

Sucking air between his teeth, Aster mentioned something about "pleasing the court." He studied the panel of four blank-faced men and eight women. "Ladies and gentlemen, I am here today to show you without a doubt that the defendant who is seated before you now was the sole cause of the ghastly murders of two men. One of whom was shot to death while fighting to rescue the very woman who'd been taken by Gary Whitehall. This is the same man who'd sworn before a United States justice to uphold, with honor and above reproach, the very laws that he himself later broke." He returned to his seat, and Riley looked across the aisle at those same beady eyes and shook his head.

"Bravo," he began, "bravo, Attorney Aster. May it please the court, Your Honor, that I will hereby mount a defense of my client whom I believe to be innocent of the charges levied against him. And ladies and gentlemen of the jury," he said, swaggering to the front and center, "before a handful of sand is thrown in your eyes, before that vision of truth that we're setting out to find this morning is clouded over by legal smoke and fanciful phrasing, I'll suggest something key to this case. That you ask yourselves during the course of this trial but one sole question: Is this case about murder? Is it?

"Or, perhaps, is it being driven by the embarrassment of the Bureau of Alcohol, Tobacco & Firearms? That is to say, these courts divine truth from cases that their agents present to good people like you. No one likes to be shown up, no one wants egg on their face. That notion we can all understand. After all, it's human.

"But ask yourself time and time again as we bring witnesses to the stand and evidence is entered into our legal record: Is it true? Or, are we vilifying a man who quit his job and did his best as a trained law enforcement officer to defend himself and another from being murdered in the foothills of the Sierra Nevada Mountains?"

I sat with my hands folded as Riley sat down next to me and waited for the prosecution to call its first witness. A Hispanic-sounding surname was called and the same well-built guy who had waited on me at Bishop's sporting goods store walked to the front. He took his oath administered by the bailiff and arranged himself in the witness box. The clerk assumed a casual demeanor, his head moving side to side, a silent beat playing in his head.

Aster was there to greet him, asking how his ride over from Bishop was. Riley began to lift his hand and then dropped it with a whisper in my ear. "Make sure everybody's comfy there, Myer."

The defendant was directed to recall the sale of the 20-gauge, everything about the transaction he could recall. There'd been my presentation of the ATF credential, although, as Aster pointed out to the jury, I had absconded by that time from my duties.

"Still, by law, an employee of the bureau," Riley interrupted.

"Counsel," the magistrate breathed into her microphone, "let the man finish. You'll get your turn." A few voices in the courtroom snickered.

"Anyhow, what I can recall," the young man continued in very good English, "was that he identified himself as ATF. And that scared me. Then he said he needed the gun and that it was strictly for sporting purposes. I thought he told me he was going after deer. Yes, I'm certain of it. He said deer because I remember wondering if he would buy the rifled slugs to go with that in order to take a deer in the mountains." A bill of receipt was produced by Aster that Riley agreed to admit as evidence. "But one last thing," the salesman added, "he said the woman he was with in the store was his wife."

"Is she in the courtroom now?" Aster countered. The record was made to show that he pointed to Liz, identifying her by hair color and dress, and a murmur went around the room.

Riley marched to the stand where Aster had been. "Mr. Ortiz, you're employed in a store that is a licensed Federal Firearms dealer, is that correct?" Ortiz nodded. "And how many years or months do you have selling firearms?"

"Eighteen months this week, sir," he said.

"Okay, eighteen months. Hmm. So you know a few things about firearms, I assume?" Again, the man dipped his chin in agreement. "Do you mind telling members of the jury—I know this is just an opinion, that you're not a firearms expert, that I have no wish to waste the court's time in bringing one in—but can you tell us all how a single shot youth gun might fare in a gun battle against two gunmen armed with semiautomatic pistols?"

Aster coughed and rose upward. "Objection, Your Honor, Mr. Ortiz was brought here to testify to a transaction in which the defendant misrepresented himself, not to testify as a firearms expert!"

"Overruled, counselor," she replied with a flip of her hand, "allow the witness to answer. This may be material to the circumstances. Go ahead, Mr. Ortiz, finish your statement if you don't mind."

"Well, Your Honor, I think it wouldn't be good. That type of shotgun can only shoot maybe 50 yards with accuracy. The pistol is much greater obviously, to say nothing of its firing capability. Your single shot, Your Honor, it must be broken down and reloaded after each shot. It's no good for a gun battle that I see police involved in."

Riley spun around. "No further questions."

"Mr. Ortiz," Aster called from where he stood, "the maximum lethal range of that shotgun? What would that be?"

"It's hard to say, sir. I'm guessing one hundred yards, maybe one fifty." His voice carried an apology in it.

"To restate, then. From one hundred and fifty yards—that's four hundred and fifty feet—our defendant might have killed the victims in this case. Thank you, Mr. Ortiz. No further questions, Your Honor."

For some reason, Aster felt the Bally's clerk should have received a full confession from us at check-in. Apparently, we failed to share with the casino employee everything that had transpired in the mountains on the night in question. Yes, the clerk admitted, the defendant's hand was cut, and yes, the defendant was treated on-site, but there had been no request for police to be called from either of us that night at the front desk.

"Are you a police officer, Mr. Simmons?" Riley asked.

"I'm a reservations agent from Bally's here in town, sir," he said in the effeminate voice I remembered.

"Exactly!" Vern shouted. "Nothing further here, Your Honor." And with that, the clerk was dismissed to Riley's eye roll.

Myer Aster pinned his index finger to his tablet and asked that the court call Mr. William Williams. A Marshal stepped into the foyer and brought in Billy wearing a churlish suit, his tie missing, a sneer buried in an untamed beard. He stalked his way through the room, swung open the half door, and threw a glare at me as he passed. A Budweiser gut shifted beneath the suit as he was sworn in and sat down. "State your name for the court, sir," Aster requested.

"Bill, William. William Williams. Friends call me Billy," he said into the mic.

Myer turned toward the courtroom and tipped his head at the ceiling, his fingers folded in some devout show, not unlike a eulogy. "Mr. Williams, can you tell the court today what your relationship was with Stanley Gorman and Ronald Borrell?"

"They was friends," he growled, "brothers in arms. Club members for life, and Stan was our leader before this guy shot him down in cold blood!" His finger pointed at me.

"Objection, Your Honor! That's hearsay," Vern yelled before

he was out of his chair. "This witness is hostile. Furthermore, he's apparently on the government's list to verify that Stanley Gorman and Mr. Borrell were killed during their vicious attack on my client. If that's the case, we'll concede that point in the prosecution's spotty evidence here, and move on!"

The judge looked angry. "Mr. Riley, need I remind you that, as an attorney practicing in this court, such outbursts are unjustified. It's understood that the court is hearing an emotionally charged witness."

Billy sat grinning as she turned to him. "And as for you, Mr. Williams, please don't draw any more conclusions about one's guilt here today. That is up to the jury to decide." Billy hunched down, drawing his hands to a fold. "Your witness, Mr. Aster."

"Thank you, Your Honor. I'll try to remove the spots from my case as has been suggested here by the defense, ladies and gentleman." Someone behind me snickered. "Mr. Williams, in your organization, would you call Mr. Gorman a leader?"

"Absolutely."

"And Mr. Borrell?"

"Well, sort of. Ron was a little wild but a good guy. One time I was alone, all the way down in L.A. My bike was broke down on the Grapevine, and a rival gang come up on me. And I give thanks to the Lord to this day that Ronnie was riding through that same day, just an hour behind me."

"And he came to your aid, did he?"

"Wiped 'em out," Billy bragged. Feet shuffled in the rear of the courtroom, and murmurs rippled through.

"Order," the magistrate called. "So, Mr. Williams, he assaulted these men who threatened you? Is that what you're telling the court?"

Billy's eyes darted back and forth. "I'll say . . . counseled them, Your Honor." Several hoots rose in the back and she tapped her gavel, glaring at the bikers. "But honest, ma'am, I got back to Bakersfield in one piece because of Ron, no matter how you say it."

"Very well," she said, noting something on paper, "go on."

"So, you had two close friends who were murdered the night in question, is that safe to say?" Aster continued.

"Yeah. Fact is, I choked up that night when word come down. Hell, we all did and we had a toast to Stan and Ron. Wasn't a dry eye in the clubhouse, I kid you not. So, yeah, we lost some good ones alright. And I know, I know, everybody's gonna say I moved into the President's rank for the power, but I'd rather it be Stan any day of the week. He had real skills for . . . leadership. Put it that way."

Myer looked pleased and made a noise with his teeth, moving in front of us and draping a hand at the jury stand divider. "So, we have two men, though with some past records—let's be fair. But two men shot down in their primes. And sitting here is Gary Whitehall, who, until just several weeks ago ran away, free to go under the banner of justice." The prosecutor waved his hand at me.

A chorus of boos rang out. Riley stood up. "Your Honor, is there a question here? Because I'm hearing nothing but posturing and badgering of my client." More boos, even louder, the crowd was getting loose, egged on by the Red Hawks.

The gavel fell, and the magistrate raised her voice. "Order! Now, for the rest of today's hearing, if there continues to be catcalls and interruptions, I'll leave it to my Marshals and bailiff to remove the source of this court's antagonism. That is my last warning." A hush fell and she smirked at Aster. "Can we hear an examination of your witness, Counsel, or are you finished?"

Billy jerked his chair and pointed an angry finger at me. "And he stole from us, Your Honor! Over one hundred thousand dollars in cash!"

"Mr. Williams, sit down!" she cried. Billy complied, falling back into his chair. "Counsel, are you aware of this allegation?"

Aster looked sick, backpedaling toward his table. "It wasn't part of my case's prosecution. I move for a recess, Your Honor, so I might have the benefit of counsel with this witness."

"Overruled. He's your witness," she said over a cupped microphone. "So, you can proceed. Frankly, I haven't heard any groundbreaking evidence from this witness, Mr. Aster." I could hear every word from where I was sitting.

"Exception," Aster said, his lips cracking dry. "May I approach the bench, Your Honor?"

"Exception noted," she answered, "and yes, you may."

Riley was at Aster's side right then, hands propping back his suit jacket to his hips. Riley strode back to our table and began writing on his tablet while Aster stood up there waving his hands.

"Oh, we got a live one, partner," Vern whispered to me as he scribbled, beads of sweat at his gray temples. He paused for a second. "That's what you're paying me with, isn't it? No—don't answer that." He looked back at the paper with a shake of his tiny head. "I don't want to know."

"No further questions," Myer uttered as he stepped back from the well. An assistant of his flipped rapidly through a legal handbook.

"No further questions, *Your Honor*," she retorted.

"Ohhh," a chorus of female voices hummed. I took distinct note of her name's placard on the bench just then, Sandra O'Kells.

"Yes, Your Honor," Myer corrected. "My apology to the bench."

Riley patted me on the knee. "Music to my ears," he whispered. "Myer just screwed up. Tell me quickly before she calls us, where'd you find that money?"

I leaned into Riley's ear and whispered, "East of Bakersfield, buried in an orange grove. Liz knew right where it was, said it was Stan's money to buy more chemicals for the cooks and sometimes—"

"Defense, your witness," the magistrate said, flicking her eyes at the women who had responded. Riley and I both froze. "Mr. Riley." The judge sounded irritated.

"Yes, Your Honor. Thank you." He crossed the court and bumped the witness stand, where Billy slouched with crossed arms. "I know this is unpleasant, Mr. Williams. And I know that you don't care much for me, I can tell. And that's okay because—"

The magistrate sighed. "Counsel," she began in a motherly tone, "please don't goad the witness. We've had enough outbursts for one day."

"Yes, Your Honor," he replied, stepping away from the stand. "Now, Mr. Williams. This one hundred thousand dollars," he repeated, clearing his throat. "Let's talk about that. Would you agree, Mr. Williams, that that's a lot of money?" Riley opened his hands and let his shoulders slump. "And, Your Honor, the relevancy here rests on the victim's motivation to kill Gary Whitehall."

Silence fell across the courtroom. Billy glared at Riley. "Yeah. It is."

Riley glanced at the notebook once more. "This, uh," he began, "great sum of cash that you claim was stolen: Was there a police report filed on the theft there in Kern County?"

"I don't know," Billy grumbled.

"If we check records for such a claim with the Bakersfield Police Department, maybe the Sheriff's office, would we find any documents at all that support what you're telling us here to today?" Riley's voice had become cutting, brief to a sharpened point.

"I tell you I don't know," Billy repeated.

"That's interesting," Vern said, tipping his head and wiping his mouth in a gesture of contemplation. "Hmm. Hundred thousand dollars lost, and we don't want a report filed. Hmm. You didn't want a report filed because you know that money came from the sales of methamphetamine, isn't that right, Mr. Williams?" The question was fired off in a declarative. "Isn't it?"

To see a man Billy's size squirm, much less in an ill-fitting suit, was strange. "Don't know," he croaked.

"Objection, Your Honor," Aster cried. "Counsel's leading my witness."

The magistrate frowned. "Sustained. Mr. Riley, the witness indicated he did not know. That's good enough. Let's just move on without any more unjustified conclusions."

Vern nodded at her. "Yes, Your Honor. And now, Mr. Williams, where was this money taken from, your club's treasury?"

Billy looked toward the back of the room, a nervous glance for cues on answering. It was clear Aster had not prepared his witness because the prosecutor sat bolt upright, leaning toward Billy with hopeful eyes flattening to little slits. Billy grunted and leaned into the microphone. "No. It was buried."

"Buried?" Riley mocked. "Like out at sea? Like a pirate's treasure, maybe?" Riley's gestures were loose, his confidence unflappable.

"In the ground, outside of town," Billy said.

Aster squirmed, Riley saw, and I think I caught Riley winking at Aster. "In the ground. So, ladies and gentlemen of the jury, let's consider this for a moment. My client is being charged with a double murder today. He's also just been accused of grand theft, though no charges were ever filed against him—this theft . . . is hearsay.

"Considering the nature of the victims in this case, burying one hundred thousand dollars seems irregular, does it not? I mean, are there any people present who have their retirement accounts buried in their backyards? After all, the Great Depression's been over now for—"

Judge O'Kells kept clicking her pen. "Mr. Riley, I'll ask you to stop with the histrionics. It's been noted that the buried cash seems irregular. But this is a murder trial, not felony theft. Proceed, now, with the witness."

"Yes, Your Honor," Riley called, striding for our table and grabbing a police report he'd been studying. "I have here in my hands, Mr. Williams, an intelligence report from the Kern County Narcotics Division in which detectives claim that Stanley Gorman was valued as a cook of methamphetamine, a process fraught with danger. Stanley Gorman, your club's president, was highly skilled—you mentioned that earlier yourself, am I right? To rephrase the question, was Stanley 'a highly skilled meth cook'? Ah—don't answer that." He spun toward the jury box and began walking toward them, snatching a separate report from the desk. "So you folks understand the legal importance of what we're talking about, allow me to share with you just two brief passages from this medical report noted in the *Journal of American Medicine.*

The magistrate cleared her throat. "Counsel, approach the bench and allow the court to preview what you're about to introduce."

Aster jumped to his feet and moved forward swiftly.

"Just defense," she waved. Aster sat back down, wringing his lips. He then turned his attention to the code book a lean gray man was pointing to. I saw Aster frown and shake his head at whatever had been found.

After a few minutes of discussion between Riley and the judge, he proceeded. "As I was saying, ladies and gentlemen, methamphetamine that we're discussing—sometimes called 'meth' or 'crystal' or 'ice'—is an extremely addictive stimulant, taking the form of a white, crystalline powder. It's taken orally, smoked, snorted, or dissolved in water and injected." Riley squinted and looked disgusted. Billy sat up there, a bear in dress clothes waiting for a question as my attorney droned on. "Now, the drug delivers to the brain an immediate, intense euphoria. Because the pleasure also fades quickly, the users often take repeated doses. The dopamine that's released heightens the experience of pleasure, hence its great street appeal."

One older woman in the back row of the jury box made a face and looked over at the witness. "Repeated methamphetamine use can easily lead to addiction—a chronic, relapsing disease characterized by compulsive drug seeking and use. This drug is rarely used medically, and then only at low doses due to its high potential for abuse. People who use this drug, you should know, may experience anxiety, confusion, insomnia, and mood disturbances and display violent behavior.

"Now, I see that confused a few of you. After all, what's this have to do with a murder? Well, later on in the trial, I intend to reference the symptoms of psychosis common with this drug. Symptoms such as paranoia, visual and auditory hallucinations, and delusions. Some users even report the sensation of insects crawling under the skin.

"We also need to understand how it's made. Currently, California authorities are uncovering numerous small clandestine laboratories with relatively inexpensive over-the-counter ingredients such as pseudoephedrine, a common ingredient in cold medicines. That sounds innocent enough, right? I have a sniffle, I'll just pop a cold tablet." He shrugged and I watched Aster slough down in his seat. "But folks, production also involves very hazardous chemicals. These chemicals can remain in the environment around a production lab long after the lab has been shut down. It's terrible and can cause a wide range of health problems for people living in the area."

I heard a chair move to my right. "Objection, Your Honor. What's the point of Mr. Riley's science report?"

"Overruled," she said. She talked with a hand at her chin, a pen cradled in her fingers. "The court finds it relevant since the victims in this case have documented ties to the drug, and, with your permission, I'd like members of the jury to understand elements that may or may not be tied to the murders of those two men."

"Of course, Your Honor, withdrawn." Myer relented.

With a nod from the magistrate, Riley turned once more to the jury. "The Prosecutor's point is duly noted, folks. I'll wrap it up. Just understand that taking even small amounts of methamphetamine can result in many of the same physical effects as those of other stimulants, such as cocaine or amphetamine. The telltale increased wakefulness, increased physical activity, decreased appetite, increased respiration, rapid heart rate, irregular heart-beat, increased blood pressure, and increased body temperature, are all negative consequences for physical health, including extreme weight loss, severe dental problems, and skin sores caused by scratching." He mock-scratched his cheek, then turned back toward Billy.

"So, Mr. Williams, in light of this information, was Stanley Gorman a meth cook, a street provider of this very dangerous drug?"

He leaned in and said flatly, "No, he wasn't. He was a leader and a friend, and that's it."

"A leader and a friend, you say?" Riley retorted. "Ah, I see. Okay, then allow me to ask this question: Did you know or were you aware of your leader's pending drug and gun charges at the time of his death?"

Billy hesitated again. "Uh, yes, I was."

"And with Mr. Borrell, his role in the club was, what did you say? I know you mentioned him helping you out of a roadside fracas. But what was his function in the Red Hawks Motorcycle Club?"

He squirmed and looked a little uneasy. "Sergeant at Arms."

Vern harrumphed and stood in the well then tipped his head at the jury. Reading from his notebook, he glanced over his glasses at Billy. "Are you aware that your friend and club officer had a rather extensive criminal background, including a murder charge from 1987 that was dropped?"

"Objection, Your Honor. The deceased victim's record is irrelevant in this matter." On his feet, Myer crossed his arms.

The magistrate paused, looked down, and pursed her lips. "Sustained. You don't have to answer that, Mr. Williams. Move on, Mr. Riley."

He pulled at his collar and looked confused. "No further questions, Your Honor." When he sat down, Vern looked a little whipped and I saw several jury members watching him. Billy left the stand, and in seconds was replaced by Keith Stubbs, who'd been waiting in the foyer.

"State your name and occupation, for the record, sir," Aster began with a confident wave of the hand.

"Keith Stubbs, Special Agent, Bureau of Alcohol, Tobacco & Firearms, Enforcement Division. I am employed by the Treasury's Fresno office, a field office of the Bureau's San Francisco regional office." Stubbs wore a navy suit not unlike my own. The slicked back hair, mawkish nose, needling eyes—a countenance hard to forget. He made no eye contact with me.

I leaned into Vern's ear, whispering, "This won't be good." He patted my hand and furrowed his brow as if to say *nothing to it.*

But I was right, Aster had worked with Stubbs, and any ground the prosecution had lost with Billy was recouped with Stubbs. He knew how to testify without feeling, as evidenced in the texture of his voice. I heard him tell the court I'd threatened him at the steakhouse, lied to him during the Gorman investigation, and denied having knowledge of Leslie Harlan's whereabouts following Gorman's arrest. It was all on record as he pointed out.

What's more, the supervisor's final report on the matter verified that I had left my job without proper notification and had confirmed over the telephone with a Bakersfield Police Department detective that not only did I know where Leslie Harlan was, but that we were leaving the area together. I kept writing on the tablet, watching Keith's expressions. As a final blow, Agent Stubbs told the court that he'd been present when I had threatened to assault Gorman while the defendant had been in custody and "helpless in handcuffs." That phrase caused a stir in the rear of the courtroom.

Stubbs produced his report of the incident, sharing a copy with Vern before reading it aloud to the court: "Your Honor, I'm sorry to read this in mixed company," he began. She nodded as he cleared his voice. "At that time, Agent Whitehall was asked for his last name by the defendant in custody. To which Gary Whitehall replied, 'None of your fucking business. That's my name, asshole. So shut the hell up before I knock your rotten teeth down your throat!'" Stubbs folded the paper.

"That ain't right!" someone yelled from the back.

"Order!" Judge O'Kells called, slamming the gavel.

Vern Riley was already on his feet when Myer Aster told the court there'd be no further questions from the prosecution. Aster beamed at the star witness, folding his hands in a prayerful manner on the way back to the table.

"Mr. Stubbs," Vern began, "great testimony today." Stubbs dipped his chin. I made more notes the more I thought about what I'd just heard. "Tell me, Agent Stubbs, did Agent Whitehall during the time of your work relationship, ever request that he be transferred to another training officer?"

"Yes, he did."

"And isn't it a fact that prior to ever meeting ATF Agent Gary Whitehall you told your office supervisor that you did not even want to supervise an agent just coming on board? That, to quote you, he'd be 'a clumsy trainee just following me around'? Isn't that how you phrased it?"

Stubbs tipped his head back and rolled his neck. I saw a flash of those rat teeth. I could tell he wanted to smart back. He cleared his throat. "I may have said something that the efficiency of my investigations at that time might suffer if I had to take time away from them in order to train a new agent, yes. Yes, I did. Our work is very labor intensive, and distractions aren't part of—"

"Distractions?" Riley repeated. "Distractions? Helping a fellow agent is a distraction to you, Agent Stubbs?"

He nodded. "It can be."

Riley examined his tablet. "Now, you mentioned that Agent Whitehall threatened you, is that correct?"

"Yes, sir, it is."

"Tell me this, though. Did he threaten you, really, or did he simply ask you to stop talking about his wife at the time?" When Riley asked that question, I saw the magistrate scrunch her nose at the witness.

Stubbs unfolded his hands and lowered the leg that had been crossed on a knee. "His wife was suffering from what Agent White-hall himself described as alcohol abuse at the time. I was simply trying to help."

"But you just said," Riley fired right back, "you just said that you had all of these high priority cases and that even working with Agent Whitehall was a distraction—or could be. It's hard for me to believe that all of a sudden you were able to commit time to someone who had no bearing on any of your cases—on her program of rehabilitation."

"Well," Stubbs said, "we didn't want to see Gary—Agent White-hall—become distracted by personal issues at home."

"Ah," Vern said with a grin, "so you were concerned or you weren't, which is it?"

Stubbs leaned toward Vern. "Yes, Attorney Riley, I was concerned. I was responsible to some degree for Agent Whitehall's performance, and I saw firsthand how his wife's personal drinking affected his performance as well as his decision to become involved with Leslie Harlan. He lied repeatedly to me, to us, about not seeing her."

Riley turned to the jury, his back to Stubbs as though he weren't listening. He kept nodding. "So, we've learned from you,

Mr. Stubbs," he said, wheeling around, "that you met a young agent who appears to have had mixed emotions about not only the nature of his work but the relationship with you. And at home, he suffered from a wife whose drinking, as you've characterized it here, was somewhat out of control?"

Stubbs deferred and said, "In so many words, I suppose."

"Tell me, Agent Stubbs," Riley continued, "did Gary ever seem stressed out to you, worried about his issues at home, anything that might cause him to lose his sense of good judgment?"

Stubbs shrugged. "Yes, I would admit that, especially after the arrest."

"Whose arrest?"

"His wife's arrest. Or at least, she was stopped for drunk driving and was able to get out of it. And to answer the question directly, Agent Whitehall did admit that he'd been bothered by the need to get her some help."

Riley clapped his hands together. "Ah, so now we have a new agent whose wife's been arrested for drunk driving. What was your solution to that, that is, as his training agent?"

"My response was two-fold, sir," Stubbs answered. "One, I suggested that my wife reach out to his wife, and two, that Agent Whitehall stay in the Bakersfield area and work on the Gorman investigation."

I turned around and caught Liz looking at me. "Hmm," Riley countered, "so the very thing that you're criticizing the defendant for—getting involved with a confidential informant and leaving with her without the permission of ATF—may have been initiated by you assigning him to an area where the source of his temptation was greatest and that—"

"Hold on, Counselor," Stubbs flashed, "Agent Whitehall was a sworn agent of the Bureau of ATF. He'd been trained on the handling of confidential informants and the level of appropriate behavior that is expected from an agent."

"Sounds mechanical, Agent Stubbs. No consideration for the human side of a young agent."

"Yes, we counseled him, told him over and over to watch himself, documenting it all, as it's written in that report. We even took him off the case to separate those two!"

"That's fine, Agent Stubbs. You did a good job in trying to handle Agent Whitehall, although do you have any regrets at all that—ah, strike that question, please. Your Honor, I have no further questions for this witness." She looked at Aster, who shook his head.

* * *

Vern Riley and I ate tuna fish sandwiches during the recess, a Marshal standing over us in a conference room while we picked at a bag of chips and sipped sodas. The morning, Vern assured me, had gone as he'd expected. Aster, he winced and said, was sure to come out firing in the afternoon.

As we were escorted back to court, I saw Liz looking at me, her female escort guiding her back in. When I smiled at her, I thought I caught her look away. My attention was forced back to the proceedings as Deputy Pinelli from the Inyo County Sheriff's Department took the stand in full khaki uniform, shocks of dark bangs combed across his head. His face pockmarked with acne scarring, Pinelli looked to be trembling, his long arms clutching the witness bannister.

Pinelli, it seemed obvious, possessed neither the poise nor the speaking skills of Keith Stubbs. Upon Aster's prompting, Pinelli confirmed that he had responded the night of the shooting and at the cabin in question had come upon "a real bloodbath." Though the judge cautioned him about inflammatory language, Pinelli then described the front of the cabin when asked about its having been "shot to bits."

Other than verifying for the jury that yes, Gorman and Borrell were dead, Pinelli moved stiffly from question to question, eyes bulging with indecision. Riley stood up at one point and reminded Pinelli that Gorman had on his person at the time of the shootings a quantity of methamphetamine, had he not? Pinelli verified that to be true through a state chemist's report, which was admitted into evidence. Vern tried to lead Pinelli into an expert's admission that the drugs in his system may have led Gorman into a drug-induced death wish, one bent on revenge. Pinelli deferred the question to Myer Aster, who objected and tossed his pencil to his table. Riley was in the well. His hands and arms hung at his side. He looked lost, standing there in silence. I wrote something else down as he began to ask Pinelli one question after another about the routine of processing a crime scene. Even to my untrained ear, it sounded like Riley was stalling, but for what, I had no idea.

I heard the shuffling of feet to my right. "Pardon me, Your Honor, but don't we have law enforcement handbooks on the outline of police procedures detailing the nature of the current cross-exam? Counsel's aim is hard to see here."

Without allowing for O'Kells's response, Vern whirled about and faced Myer. "I'm just wondering what happened to the money." He turned back to Pinelli. "Care to tell us?"

"The money, sir?"

Riley began walking and talking and waving his hands, "Yes, deputy, the money. Green stuff, cash, moolah, two thousand dollars to be exact. Sound familiar, deputy? So, tell us, Pinelli! Where'd it go?"

Pinelli's eyes opened wide and he swallowed hard. "Sir, I have no idea what you're talking about."

"I'll remind you that you're under oath, young man," Riley said, scowling while bracing his hands at the back of his chair. "My clients put two thousand dollars in an envelope, Your Honor, and left that money on the counter of that cabin in a show of good faith; that the owners of the place might be able to repair it to its original condition. And no one from Inyo County knows anything about it?" He was shouting, to a degree that his own wallet had been emptied of two grand.

"I never saw it, Your Honor," said the deputy. He looked to be telling the truth.

"That's mighty peculiar. Money marked for a specific purpose, left behind as my client then fled for his life. Law enforcement shows up, processes the scene extensively as you've just pointed out to us, details the murders, but when it comes to a fat pocketful of cash, nobody's the wiser!" Riley's face had turned scarlet.

"Objection, Your Honor!" Aster groaned. "Counsel's trying to discredit my witness."

"Sustained. Defense, do you have anything further?" Riley shook his head and laid the notebook down. "Does the prosecution wish for a recross?"

Aster raised an index finger. "No, Your Honor, but since we're on this topic and have heard this unfounded claim of Mr. Riley's, the prosecution calls the defendant's girlfriend, Leslie Harlan. She can speak to this mysterious cash, as well as the defendant's recent arrest in Ohio for assault, and most of all, the murders in this case."

A clamor arose in the rear of the courtroom when a woman's voice, singular and shrill, cut through the decorum. "Are you fucking serious?" she screamed. "She gets to testify? What about Stanley, huh? What about him!"

A man's voice answered just as I turned. It was the younger of the two Marshals, a stout man with a crew cut. His arm was extended at an older woman who was struggling beneath the embrace of one of the Red Hawks. "I don't give a damn what she says, Ricky!"

"You—out! Now!" the Marshal ordered. All eyes turned, and the gravity of the case, the pomp and propriety of legalese and benches and law degrees and juror opinions—all of it—turned on its head. The woman's struggle was split between the thinnest of the bikers, a man with a long angular face and greasy shag haircut, and the Marshal. No one in the room was going to deny the burly Marshal his right to evict unruly observers of the proceedings. One head that was not turned to the rear was a familiar one. It was Liz.

She mouthed *Brenda*.

Confusion swept over me, between the screaming woman, kicking and clawing her way out of the courtroom against her will, and the notion that she had once been Leslie's best friend. She looked old. But then it dawned on me. *Meth.*

The thin man who had attempted to calm her—hadn't she cried out 'Ricky'? Ricky. Telephone Ricky. The gang member the narcs had tried to frame as a snitch after the raid on Gorman's place? That was him back there alright, tall and skinny just like the photos I'd seen, minus the ponytail. And now he craned his neck toward Billy, the two of them going back and forth. The Marshal slammed open the door with Brenda in tow, and in the foyer I could see other men in blazers, other officers of the court assisting.

Seconds later, the door flew back open, and the Marshal reappeared, winded, his necktie off center. Myer Aster had risen to his feet, waving his arms at the Bench, hoping for what I wasn't sure. The Marshal marched up to the end of the last row. "That's it—all of you Red Hawk people—let's go. Show's over! Up and out. Can't have these distractions, you heard the judge. Let's go!"

He glanced at the judge who gave out a cough and spoke to the court reporter through her microphone. "Let the record show that the party of Mr. Williams was asked to leave the courtroom." Riley let his mouth hang open, pleased as could be without smiling.

Back there a small queue of bikers, Billy included, rose one by one, waving their hands in protest while the Marshal stood at the end of the bench, nodding toward the door, swinging a Maglite to show the way. Liz sat weeping. When the fracas died down, and the door closed with a seal, the courtroom was pin-drop quiet once more. We were all looking at one another as if to convey, *did that just happen?*

The bailiff stepped forward, a sheen of sweat on his forehead, his eyes bugged with anxiousness. Myer seemed confused. The bailiff stood board-straight and announced to the room without hesitation, "The prosecution has called Leslie Harlan to the stand."

Liz rose, her cheeks swollen and red, moving toward the bailiff on wobbly heels. I leaned over and whispered in Vern's ear, "Is she okay? She doesn't look so good."

Vern shot to his feet. "Your Honor, the defense moves for a recess at this time. The witness appears upset, and her testimony is crucial in this case."

The magistrate pursed her lips, looked down at her papers, then at Liz who had stepped up to be sworn in. "I'll allow for it,

Counsel. In light of all that's gone on here this afternoon, the Court will reconvene tomorrow morning at nine. And bailiff, the members of the motorcycle club will be barred from proceedings for the remainder of this trial. Let the record show. There were far too many distractions here today to continue in the same manner."

Aster had one hand on his hip, prepared to utter something that would not pass his lips, his other hand pressed to his forehead as though suffering a migraine. I thought I heard Liz thank the judge right before the bailiff roared for all of us to rise. The magistrate left the room.

Before I had a second's thought to process everything, the large black Marshal bumped me at my shoulder, instructed me to gather my things, and all but hoisted me to my feet. Riley promised to visit early in the morning as I was whisked away.

On the way to the van, a barrage of faces and voices met me, all electric with random movement and sound. Camera bulbs flashed. Over my shoulder I heard a heavy voice announce, "That's him there."

And then I was gone.

CHAPTER FIFTEEN

Even though I'd been awake since sunup, Riley broke into my room with the rush of a morning drill sergeant. It was still early. An older deputy with a bushy mustache left the door flung open and he disappeared with a jingle of keys.

"Okay, Sunshine, let's straighten that tie a little, huh? And in the meantime, I have some news for you! Remember that picture a local reporter took of you?" He rifled through his bag and in a rustle unfolded the morning's paper. On the left was my picture and on the right, one of Liz passing through a courtroom doorway. Together the two photographs held up a massive block-letter headline:

ROBIN HOOD MEETS ROMEO & JULIET

"Robin Hood?" I repeated. "What is this? Won't this hurt our—"

Vern threw up a hand and went back to his bag for a manila folder. "Not at all. Not in the slightest. That's called winning in the court of public opinion, my friend. Readers see this story and guess what? They're pulling for you. Everyone's seen this. Well, except the jury, of course. But without a doubt, from the judge to Aster on down, they've seen it. Hell, two of the deputies showed me their newspapers on my way up here this morning."

I dropped back to the bed and sighed. "So, what, Liz and I are seen as thieves, is that it?"

Riley shook his head, his eyes squeezed tight, insistent. "Wrong, wrong, wrong—you're . . . out of touch, man. The jury knows your background, they'll know Leslie's after this morning. By the way, I just met with her. She's regained her composure, very upbeat about all of this. She didn't understand until this morning that she was being granted criminal immunity in exchange for her cooperation and testimony. Carbona had agreed previously to it with Aster. She didn't know she had immunity because Carbona failed to make it clear to her at our first meeting. What a moron, that one."

I scoffed, the image of Carbona standing broad and arrogant at my trial while I faced sentencing. "So, all the marbles of their case go to efforts to get me."

"Yeah, but yesterday's testimonies—with the exception of Stubbs's—were weak. But remember something, you're not on trial for lying to your boss. If you were, half of America would be guilty, let's face it." He slapped me on the knee.

"Liz say anything else?"

He twisted his lips and stared at the floor. "Mm, no. Just that she said she can't wait to get home—"

"Whoa. Home? Hold on a second. You mean home to Ohio? She said that?"

He shrugged. "I assume so. But, now, listen to me, Gary. First things first. You two lovebirds can work out your issues once I get you out of this mess.

"On Myer's agenda for today, we're looking at Carbona's testimony off the bat. It was supposed to be Liz up first, I know, but the judge allowed for the revision since Carbona's supervising the service of an arrest warrant later this morning out in Henderson. He needs to leave. Then, after he's done and Liz finishes, it's just closing arguments. We should be done by noon, easy, I'm thinking. And no Red Hawks today."

Vern Riley was wrong—dead wrong—about the Red Hawks. A line of sign-toting bikers paraded before the courtroom that morning with officers from the Vegas PD monitoring the protest. From the van I could read one crudely-fashioned sign in gloppy red letters: GOVT PROTECTS ONE OF ITS OWN! We shot around the building and into the back entrance. The same Marshal escorted me into court, past Liz again. With her hair pulled back in neat braids, she'd been granted the privilege of wearing a second, smart dressy outfit.

There was little argument over the testimony of Agent Carbona. He came wheeling into the courtroom, tanned, looking occupied but not harried, intelligent but not ill-tempered. Once he'd been given the floor, Carbona paraphrased the Bradley Wilson report and how he'd come to be involved in the case. The Las Vegas FBI office had been delegated by Washington to investigate the ugly business of a brother agency. Carbona spoke frankly: The federal government wished to avoid any appearance of bias in the matter, to prevent "signs like the ones being carried outside the courthouse," he said with a smirk.

He revealed in conversational English that his frustration peaked when he'd gone to Flagstaff himself to question Liz and me. After a brief unsuccessful search for us about town, he made a last phone call to Karen Swayze of Flagland Realty Company. He admitted that he had expected to find us right away. After we had "absconded"—the criminal's tag at which I bristled—his investigation into the matter had been "put on the back burner."

I leaned into Vern's ear during a lull and whispered, "In other words, until Robin opened her big mouth." There had been no nationwide manhunt mounted to catch up with me, no all-points bulletins, not even a dragnet along possible highways of escape.

Vern nodded and stood up. He told the magistrate that he had no questions for Carbona. I heard Liz sigh several rows back.

As I watched her walk past in a business suit with a skirt just above the knee and low pumps, it dawned on me that my freedom hinged on the testimony she was about to give. I reminded myself in flashbacks of times when I'd been vulnerable with her. The time I'd blurted a request for her number. Sweating it out at Smith's Bakery over coffee. Her blow up over my true identity at the hotel. The parking lot scene where I showed up with a trunkful of explosives, begging for a second chance. Even the shootout at the cabin where she'd urged me to kill to Stanley. And here we were again.

Riley had already reviewed with me the Akron Police Department report that had been faxed to Carbona's office. Myer Aster introduced the document into the state's list of exhibits without protest, explaining to the judge that it, along with the testimony of my girlfriend, would help establish my "propensity for sudden and terrific violence." This was recent, this was key, and this needed to be presented to the jury, he swore.

"I'll allow it, Mr. Aster," the judge said, "but only within those parameters. There'll be very little latitude. You're not going to bring up parking tickets the defendant received in Ohio to show he's a reckless driver."

He nodded and turned to face Liz head on. His eyes burned into hers, the body language of a hypnotist. "Miss Harlan, you and you alone are the only person—beside the defendant himself—who was present at the bar fight on your last night in Akron that is detailed in this report. Now, I need you to tell us what happened right from the beginning, okay? So . . . you two had been involved in your spree of violence and had fled from justice and wound up drinking in this Bucket Shop beer joint and—"

Vern slid his chair back from the table. "Objection, Your Honor. Prosecution's not only starting out leading this witness, he's editorializing the case and putting words in her mouth. 'Spree of violence,' Prosecutor?"

"Mr. Riley, I will address the parties in this courtroom, thank you. And you, Mr. Aster, perhaps allowing the witness to explain to the jury what happened of her own volition might benefit all involved. Understand?"

"Yes, Your Honor," Aster answered. "Miss Harlan?"

Liz looked at the jurors, glanced at me and Vern, and wet her lips. "Well, it happened like this. Gary was there when I arrived and was talking to his wife—well, they're separated right now. I'd just gotten off work and went over just because he left me a note saying that we were going to celebrate. It said he had big news."

Aster cut in. "What was the news that night?"

She flared her eyes. "I don't know. I never did find out. As soon as the fight was over, we were separated by police. At the hospital Gary said we would talk about it later."

"I see. So, there you are, just getting off work. You're invited across the street to this bar to celebrate something, and you get there and Gary is there with his wife and—"

"He wasn't with her. He was standing there talking to her," Liz said. My left hand was busy scratching out a few notes. "And he looked uncomfortable to me, like he didn't want to talk to her, at least in front of me. To be honest, I wasn't sure which. So, we were introduced. Her name's Robin, and drinks were ordered. I think she'd been drinking before I got there because she seemed drunk to me at that point.

"So, I sat down and that's when she accused me of breaking up her marriage. She called me a few names that I can't repeat—"

Aster unfolded his arms and motioned toward her. "Miss Harlan, I need you to tell us exactly what was said. That's the point of a trial."

"Okay," she said, clearing her throat. "Well, I knew she had a drinking problem. Gary had told me that when we were out in California. Anyway, she called me 'a whore' and something else she said other ATF agents told her about me."

"ATF?" Aster yelped. His face cringed. "What are you saying?"

"I'm just telling you what she said," Liz replied. "She said those agents from California had told her about me. That's what she said. Those were the words she used, 'They told me all about you.' She used the expression 'biker slut' at one point, but I can't remember if that's what they said or it was just something she came up with at the time. It all happened so fast."

Aster shook his head, glancing at Riley and clenching his teeth. He stood erect and faced Liz once more. "Okay, then what?" He looked fearful.

"Well, I said something I shouldn't have. I was on the defense, you understand, and so I mentioned to her how I . . . heard . . . that she threw up all the time, 'cause of her drinking. And she called Gary a murderer and then he told her to shut up and grabbed her by the arm." She reached for her own arm. "Like this. Then Robin's boyfriend came running over with his friend and that's when the fight broke out."

The room was quiet, I noticed, far more than it had been at any other time during the trial. Aster waved at her. "Just a second,

Miss Harlan. Now this part is very important. Explain, if you will, the assault on this Mr. Raff. How did that happen exactly?"

She resettled herself in the chair and touched her hair. "Well, like I said, it was fast. But I remember him grabbing Gary, and Robin got shoved against the wall. And this guy had Gary in a bear hug and he was a pretty big guy. I saw Gary's face right then. He looked scared. Because the other guy was coming around the bar, too. That's when it happened."

"What happened?"

She raised her right arm and swooshed it through the air in a hooking motion. "Gary went like this with the glass in his hand and he hit the guy in the back of the head with it. I remember 'cause ice flew up. And then that guy fell down and Gary was standing there, and I saw that his hand was bleeding but he still had the broken glass bottom in his hand. Then the other guy looked like he was going to punch Gary, but Gary waved the glass at him. Then that guy stopped coming at him and just yelled at him to get out, and so did the bartender. She said she'd called the cops, so I figured I should leave, and I did.

"And at the apartment across the street, Gary showed up and his hand was bleeding and then, two minutes later, if that, the cops came to the door."

Aster began nodding. "So, Gary hit one man savagely with a broken glass and was prepared to wound another when the police were notified?"

Liz paused, still. She raised her eyebrows at Aster. "Well, sort of, yeah."

Riley tossed his pen down and made a face at Aster. The judge furrowed her brow at Riley, and he put up his hands and smiled falsely. Several jurors noticed.

Aster continued. "Thank you, Miss Harlan. Now, the prosecution would like to know about the cash that was mentioned yesterday. Please tell us where you got it and how much was involved."

She shook her head, eyes blind of feeling, blue reflections showing Aster nothing. "There wasn't any money."

"No money?"

"No." She looked at him with lifeless eyes. My stomach tightened.

The attorney pressed his lips with his index and middle fingers and flipped through notes, speaking as he rattled through pages in his notebook. "Now, I want to remind you of several things today, Miss Harlan. One," he shouted, raising an index finger toward the ceiling, "you are under oath. Two," he continued as a second finger joined the first, "you have agreed to cooperate fully with the government in exchange for criminal immunity—"

Riley wheeled into the aisle, standing center room. "Your Honor, we object. Mr. Aster is provoking this witness who, I should add, has been very cooperative up to this point. Furthermore, this phantom money he's talking about is all based on hearsay. As we heard yesterday, the claim was made by a witness whose credibility in a court of law is questionable, at best. It's unsubstantiated, Your Honor. No police report, no documents, just a witness who is motivated by revenge. I move that this missing money be stricken from the record.

"After all, I am here to defend Gary Whitehall on the charge of murder, not to recount what happened in an Ohio bar, not to explain away missing cash that a criminal enterprise says was his doing." Riley stopped cold, his hands on his hips.

The judge raised her pen to make a point. "Sustained, Counsel. We'll leave the testimony and line of questioning stand. Miss Harlan just denied the money's existence. So, let's move on, Mr. Aster."

"Miss Harlan," Aster shouted, "did Gary Whitehall shoot Stanley Gorman and Ronnie Borrell?"

A murmur rippled through the courtroom and a hush fell. Liz moved in her seat, arms fixed to the chair's armrests. "Well . . . yes, he did."

"Ah! Now, we're getting somewhere. I noticed you paused, Miss Harlan. Why is that? Are you trying to protect Gary Whitehall in these proceedings?"

My breathing slowed, shallow and dry. Jurors glanced at me. Liz spoke up. "No, I'm not, sir."

Aster stood there studying her, arms folded before the witness stand. Liz never blinked but sat there staring back, her lips undisturbed.

The prosecutor said, almost at a murmur, "You realize, Miss Leslie Harlan, that you are defending a married man today, a man whose wife in Ohio is currently expecting his child?"

My heart leaped into my throat. *Robin!* Vern jumped up, the judge turned her head and squinted at Aster, and those in the courtroom gave out a collective "ohh!"

"Answer me, Miss Harlan."

Liz looked at me, her face wounded. She swallowed. "Yes."

Vern had heard enough. He protested, and the judge allowed for the question to stand along with her response. The sickening question caused me to tremble visibly. Vern saw and sat down, placing his arm behind me and leaning in. "Take it easy," he whispered, his voice dark, his eyes shifting across the jury box. "Don't let them see you sweat it. Is that true, is she?"

I shook my head. "No. Hell no," I murmured. "She's a liar."

The judge instructed Aster to direct his questions toward the charge itself, that her courtroom would not be turned into a soap opera. Myer strutted before the jury and wheeled back toward Liz. "So, Miss Harlan, here's you and this married man holed up in a remote cabin. It says in the Inyo County report that your former live-in boyfriend sustained multiple gunshot wounds to both the head and chest that night. Now, tell us something. Did the defendant here, did he really need to keep firing these—what are they called?—ah, 'rifled slugs.' Did he, in your opinion, need to keep firing one slug after another into the victim?"

Liz shook her head and tucked loose hair behind her ear. "I don't know. I guess not." She looked empty up there, her face an ash color. Robin. I scratched out a few more notes, glancing at Liz from my chair.

"Did Gary shoot all the rounds from the cabin?"

She sighed. "I don't remember. Maybe he stood over him after Stan was . . . down. I can't recall."

"He stood over him and fired his weapon into a dead man!" Aster raised his arms in alarm at the jury.

I buzzed into Vern's ear. "That's not true. I kicked him but the last shot I fired came from the cabin."

Aster raged on. "And all so he could have you for himself, to keep you from law enforcement, to go on the run, to return to Ohio, where he continues a . . . "

"Counsel," the judge warned, her voice slanted with temperament.

"Yes, Your Honor. Now Miss Harlan, why did Gary Whitehall kill those two men the night of May 22nd? Can you tell us that?"

She blinked at the prosecutor and moved her mouth in a mechanical way. "He said he loved me and that he wanted to run away to another state."

"He loved you enough to kill for you," he said. Aster folded his arms. "After he took you away from the cabin, did he ever discuss how to avoid apprehension by law enforcement?"

Liz whispered, "Yes."

"I'm sorry, I didn't hear you."

"Yes!" Her face shaded to pink.

"If he was innocent, did he ever talk about turning himself in?"

"Huh uh," she said and she righted her posture. "No, he was worried about the gang catching up to us. Them and the FBI. We'd seen the news reports."

"So, former Agent Whitehall knew that the FBI wanted him for questioning, and he willfully evaded them?"

She rocked her head up and down. "Said they weren't going 'to throw him in some Vegas lockup while they got their shit together.'" Her voice sounded icy, indifferent. *They're going to convict me of murder.*

Aster clapped his hands together. "I have no further questions for this witness, Your Honor."

"Mr. Riley, your witness."

Riley rose up, his fingers tapping on our table and I scratched away at my pad. "Miss Harlan," he began, "did Stanley Gorman ever threaten you or abuse you physically during the time in which you were his live-in girlfriend?"

Her eyes lowered. She nodded. "Yeah—yes, he did."

"And did Gary Whitehall defend you from Stanley Gorman the night of the shootings?"

"Yes."

"Did he ever pursue either Stanley Gorman or Ronnie Borrell—outside the scope of his duties as an ATF agent?"

She looked over at the jury and then back at Vern. "No, sir. He just wanted to get away. It was all planned out."

Vern rubbed his face. "Did he sit up there in the cabin waiting for assassins or bad men to show up?"

"No," she said. "He turned his gun in to ATF when he left his car in Bakersfield. In fact, he didn't even want a gun up there at the cabin. I was the one who told him to buy the gun he used that night because I knew the gang would come looking for us after we left town together. And I was right."

Riley smiled. "Ah. Good decision. Without your suggestion, who knows?" Liz let her eyelids close and simpered. He moved close to her. "So, are we safe to tell the jury that this was a case of self-defense?"

"Yes, definitely."

"Thank you, Miss Harlan. Thank you. I have nothing further for this witness, Your Honor."

The judge slid her papers into a single sheaf and nudged the frame of her glasses to the bridge of her nose. "You may step down, Miss Harlan." Liz pushed herself upward and moved through the courtroom while we all studied her carriage, her eyes, facial expression. Nothing.

"Mr. Aster, your closing remarks?"

"Thank you, Your Honor," Myer said. The courtroom grew quiet. The attorney strode toward the jury box. One juror, a large man with a wolfish face, sighed and refolded his hands across his belly. Outside the courtroom a siren passed by. "Ladies and gentlemen, justice demands that we determine here whether or not Gary

Whitehall was responsible for the murders of Stanley Gorman and Ronnie Borrell. Did he pull the trigger? Yes, he did. Did he kill not one but two human beings? Yes, he did.

"You see, all the characteristics of someone capable of murder are in place here. He left his agency in a lurch, one. He lied to his supervisors again and again. As an agent, he was counseled again and again on not seeing Leslie Harlan. Did he heed those warnings? No, he did not. In fact, this man swore up and down that he was not seeing her romantically when the record shows that he was. Furthermore, he'd been plotting all along to abscond with her like an infidel. He stole away another man's girlfriend, the very man he helped arrest earlier that very day. Just imagine it!

"He usurped the power vested in him as an agent of the Bureau of Alcohol, Tobacco & Firearms for his own means. All to run off with a strange woman when his wife of record struggled at home with alcohol abuse. You have to ask yourself, 'Does this even sound like a federal agent?' A position associated with excellence in enforcement of our country's highest laws? Out of respect to the court, I'll not accuse him of stealing black market cash." Aster glanced at the bench just then. The judge was reading something.

"Otherwise, we're looking at a man who, in a matter of days went from one of the country's most respected lawmen to a thief and a murderer. How do I make such a claim, one might ask? Simple. Liars cannot be trusted. You heard the testimony. He lied to the gun dealer. He lied to his supervisor. He had a chance to report the murders at the hotel but he chose to hide those. The FBI came knocking and he ran.

"We know he's capable of violence. Think back to his supervisor. And then, the night of his arrest in Akron, where he smashed a man over the head with a glass, threatening still another with broken shards." I looked down at my hand, its scar still purple in its healing. A woman juror caught me looking at it.

"Jurors, it will be up to you now, to set the record straight, to convict this man so that the United States government can see justice through. Gary Whitehall shot those men. Period." He threw back his head and whispered that he had nothing more to offer the court.

"Mr. Riley, your closing, sir."

"Thank you, Your Honor," he replied, moving toward the empty witness stand with swift steps. "I'm moving over here because frankly, I don't want to be within arm's length of my client when I admit to you that Gary Whitehall is guilty." Several people behind me grumbled at Vern. The large juror tipped his head at Vern and squinted.

Vern raised his hand, his back to the stand. "He is. He is guilty. He is guilty of lying to a number of people. Mr. Aster had it right. And, he's also guilty of adultery. That much is true, too. He left his own wife for a woman who, until that time, was living with another man. Lastly, he'll admit to anyone who asks that he's guilty of stupidity as well." Someone in the back of the room laughed. I sighed.

"This man, ladies and gentlemen, did not even realize that the woman he loved happened to be the very girlfriend of the man he was investigating. That is, until he did surveillance at the home of Stanley Gorman and only then did he recognize the automobile of Leslie Harlan. Only then did he get it. He thought the waitress who'd been waiting on him at the Village Inn in Bakersfield had been a pretty face, a soft voice to turn to when problems at home with his own wife had driven him away. Am I building an excuse? No, of course not. But those facts seem a lot more understandable than the picture Mr. Aster just painted for you.

"And with all due respect to Your Honor," he continued, turning toward the bench for effect, "Law makes no room for love. It's true. We want facts in this place. But this man fell in love with a woman when his own home life was collapsing and he found himself ensnared in a job that he had no heart for. And this witness, Liz Harlan, has made it plain that she was abused, living in fear with a man who had a criminal record that made him the target of federal investigations.

"No, no, Stanley Gorman and Ronnie Borrell were not common drunkards being thrown out of Bakersfield's honky-tonks. No, these man were leaders in the meth trade, manufacturers. And they went after my client bent on destruction with one aim—to kill. It only takes one look at the photo exhibit of the cabin to understand how many shots were fired at Gary Whitehall and Liz Harlan.

"So, in conclusion, I'll point to my client and say, guilty. Guilty of unorthodox methods, of not owning up to the shootings, but you've got to say he's innocent of the charges here. Society is rid of two of its worst. Let's not make matters worse. That 'leadership' we heard about earlier in Mr. Williams's testimony, that's a simple euphemism for meth cook. Narcotics agents have documented reports in which Stan Gorman was pinpointed as a skilled producer of methamphetamine. A drug producer and his henchman are gone, ladies and gentlemen. Let the man who was forced to defend himself on that fatal night leave us with a silent 'thank you.' He's had enough. It's up to you now."

I heard Aster sigh to my right. He looked peaceful for once, the eyes drowsy for a change. I appreciated Riley just then, and he relented his defense. The judge ordered the jury to withdraw. I shook the hand of Vern Riley as the courtroom cleared.

CHAPTER SIXTEEN

Finally we were led back to the quiet of the waiting courtroom. Conversations buzzed behind us. I handed Vern a note and asked him to pass it on to Liz. He seemed unmoved and mumbled something about it not looking good in the eyes of the court. But he promised to give it to the lady Marshal in the back of the room, a stentorian type with severe cat-eyed glasses that gave her a matriarchal air. I glanced at it one last time and whispered, "Give it to her but tell her I know she doesn't smoke. I was just trying to make the poem work." He made a face at me, the paper folded and pinched between his fingertips.

"I'll have to read it first," he said. "We've come too far to screw this up with some courtroom shenanigans."

"If you have to," I replied. He unfolded it and spread it on the table.

Song of the Soul

The plain smells warm and the trees rise up
And form sycamore roads never dared at night
A star shines o'er Ohio's great mane of uncombed green
And grey arteries, each road stranded

A woman I knew wept sweetly in the silent silver dawn,
Puffy-eyed and smoking her distant dreams
Its cherry glowing in the dark
Once her heart was as beautiful and blue

As Sunday clouds, purple as flowers from the Plain
As significant to me as a Lake Erie teardrop
That taps upon my roof, long before the sunrise
And opening eyes of slumbering fools.

Vern sat there, his lips moving in silence, an eyebrow hooked high. He stared at me and dangled the paper from his fingers. "When did you write this?"

"When I was sitting here."

He grinned. "What the hell does it mean?"

"Just give it to her. She'll know."

And I turned and watched the animated gestures of Vern Riley handing it to the manly guard, pointing at Liz. The thing was flung open and likewise, I had to sit and watch a second uninvited reader look it over. Just before she folded it up, I thought I saw a faint smile pass her lips as she marched up the aisle. I turned back around before she reached Liz. Slumping down, I heard whispers. Riley was at my shoulder, easing down into his chair. "Why didn't you say you were a poet?" he asked with a smirk. "I would have had you write my closing."

When I was sure she'd had time to study it, I turned and saw her blue eyes look up. Tears were on her cheeks and she pawed at them with a wrist. Riley turned back around with me, stealing a look himself. "Damn, Romeo," he cracked, "that's impressive."

* * *

The bailiff threw open the door and announced the judge's entrance just before she called in the jury. Riley's small hand rested on my shoulder. "Just over fifty minutes. That's either great news, or you're going to the gas chamber and I should be disbarred."

"Hey," I shot back under my breath, "don't joke about this shit. I'm scared."

He tapped my hand. I glanced behind me. Liz had resumed the face of indifference, staring through the window. I wasn't sure who frightened me more, Liz or the military-looking jury foreman with no neck and a haircut I once heard referred to as a Chicago Box.

Some other things were said, which I ignored, waiting for the magistrate's words. "Has the jury reached a verdict?"

"We have, Your Honor. We find the defendant not guilty of the charge of murder."

Not guilty.

He just said 'not guilty.' Not guilty. Not a murderer, not a killer. Not guilty. By the time the remainder of the charges were rendered and I had Riley clutched against my chest, I understood that I had been found guilty only of obstruction of justice. The magistrate had ruled that I was given credit for my time served but that I would owe the government a fine.

"Five hundred." Riley pursed his lips with a squint. "It's nothing, man. It's nothing. You're free, Gary. Free. Have them take you back over to the jail for processing out of the system and get your things. You can catch the next flight out if you want, or stick around and play the slots. Hell, as far as the court's concerned, you can go out there and meet with the Red Hawks if you want, if they're still out there. That big Marshal back there told me one of them got arrested for disorderly conduct this morning. I thought he said they'd all but disbanded."

I clamped down on that little hand of his. Over my shoulder Myer Aster mumbled a few words of concession to Vern. When I turned to face him, he scowled and marched off.

"What's his problem?" I asked.

"Uh, he lost," Vern said. "That happens."

"Hmm. Well, Mr. Riley," I began, "I owe you big time. I still have your card, and I'll have that cashier's check for seven thousand in the mail just as soon as I get back to Akron. And I just thought of something else. Now that we're in the clear with the justice system, I can write to Karen Swayze and get our deposit back."

"Who's Karen Swayze?"

"Oh, she's the real estate agent Carbona mentioned—remember? We rented a house through her down in Flagstaff. I held off on getting my deposit back—it's a long story—but she owes Liz and me five hundred bucks, and so that can cover my fine."

Riley leaned in and whispered, "I can get the court's journal entry when it's available and send it back with a letter to the Akron courts. You know, to show that your trouble back there in that bar was a case of self-defense."

"That'd be great. Get me off the docket for the assault charge."

He was folding up things, dog-eared folders and notebooks he crammed back into his briefcase. He mumbled something to me, but then the Marshal appeared, his demeanor loose. "You ready to go back now?"

"I am." I turned to Riley once more. "Thanks again, Vern."

He looked up and called at me, grinning. "See you, Whitman."

* * *

At the back of the courtroom, I saw Liz and asked for permission to speak with her. The Marshal said wryly that he had all day, why not? I turned away from him and tapped Liz on the hand as she waited on the elevator with her matron. The matron gave me a funny look, like a high school chaperone who'd been tested by a wild boy. "Where are you going now?"

She turned sidewise from me, her face strange and recalcitrant. *Had it been the poem that upset her?*

The lady Marshal spoke up, her voice soft, belying the tough look. "She'll be going back to the women's jail for her things, and then you two will be free to go."

I nodded. "So, Liz, where should we meet?"

Liz remained stiff-necked and turned away. The lady spoke right through her. "We're going all the way out near the speedway, then we'll be dropping her off at the airport. If you want to see her, then look for her at one of the gates."

Liz turned to her. "I don't want to see him," she said in measured syllables.

"What? What do you mean?" Deep in my arms, a nervous reaction shook. "What did I do?"

Behind me, the black Marshal tugged at my sleeve. "Hey, partner. Let's get moving. Ya'll can talk at the airport. You need to get your belongings from county over there."

I tore my arm away from him. "Hold on, man," I said and turned to her. "What's this all about, Liz?"

The elevator car opened its door to the foyer. She got on. And when she turned to face me, her eyes went to the marble floors of the courthouse. "I'll see you at the airport," I shouted just before the door sealed itself and groaned downward.

The Marshal and I shuffled off. "Son of a bitch. What did I do?" He was moving through the walkway, my neck and brain numb of nerve endings.

"You all will get travel vouchers now," he said. "No need for us to escort you now. You a free man." Down the steps we went, my breathing difficult in the stale air of the stairwell, each fluorescent light blinding me.

"She said she didn't want to see me," I announced, stumbling down a pair of steps and catching myself on the landing.

"Oh, and you surprised about that?" he asked, unlocking the van door. "Just buckle up is all I ask. No need for you in cuffs now." We rose into the seats, the motor fired, and I clicked the belt buckle as we roared into Vegas traffic. "They be having your vouchers at the jail. They just better."

"Hey, come again, man. What's that bit about don't be surprised? What'd you mean by that?"

He hit the signal and looked down one of the main streets, its casinos throbbing with color, even at midday. "I got to spell it out for you, huh?"

"Yeah, what are you saying right now?"

"Mm-mm-mm, I don't know what you was seeing, but from where I was standing, you had that fine lady all on your side. When Old Mr. Aster, he come with that bit about you gotta another woman pregnant, that's when it changed." He gassed it around the corner and we sailed down the boulevard, his eyes scanning the lights. "Yeah, that's when it changed. Mm hmm."

I shook my head at the passing buildings. "But see, I didn't do that. That's my wife. She's—she's a liar!"

The Marshal laughed and rolled the knob of his two-way radio to squelch the static. He had a great laugh, deep in the chest. "Do I look like the judge to you? I'm goin tell ya something. Ain't no harsher judge than a woman, you got me?" We stopped at a light. "And you got pass O'Kells today. Mm hmm. Let me tell you, that's something. 'Cause when I dragged your ass up in there yesterday morning, I had marked it with Lenny. He up in the court. I say you was 15 to 25, easy. She like you, though. I know you ATF, but hey, a crime's a crime."

"Hey, I'm one of you—us, you know. I went to agent training, all that. Don't tell me about it," I spat.

"I ain't telling you about it. You telling me. I'm just saying 'cause your lady don't look none too happy just now," he said. "But you look a straight shooter. You get past Judge O'Kells? You past the problem there. You see what I'm saying?"

I nodded. "Yeah, I guess."

*   *   *

The jail doors opened, the jail doors closed, and within the hour, I had a paper bag stuffed with belongings, including the folded suit and a government-issue shaving kit. My street clothes felt good again, though the blood on my shirt had blackened to quarter-sized blots. I had a bill faxed over from Riley, hand-delivered by Jimmy, who shook my hand as I departed. I looked at the paper. Three thousand five hundred due within thirty days. A small italicized notation: *Legal fees, single defendant Whitehall.* A second invoice for $500 due to the United States Justice Department arrived for me just before Pat Sommers, a patrol deputy, rolled up for my airport escort. A hard quiet man, he rode in silence, taking every turn on squealing wheels. At the airport, he shot up to the curb, I got out, no words were exchanged, and he tore off from the terminal.

I spotted Liz and rushed to where she was sitting, an indifferent face turned toward the terminal windows, just as it'd been in the courtroom lobby. "You get one of these?" I asked, waving the voucher. She nodded. I asked again, sensing that I had to break the bubble that surrounded her. "Huh?" I waved the voucher again. "Did you get one of these?"

"I said *yes.*"

"What, just go up there to the counter with it?" I scanned the flights on the blue board at the gate and got behind two others. Within minutes, I was booked for American Flight #248, non-stop service from Las Vegas to Cleveland International. After tearing a perforated ticket from my voucher book, the agent pointed at what she was handing back. "That's for your cab fare once you arrive in Cleveland, sir. That'll get you back to your home destination from the airport."

"Oh," I said, sighing in relief. "Thank you. So, you'll start boarding when?"

The young agent with dark glossy hair rolled her wrist to watch side up. "That flight will start boarding in just over an hour. Down the concourse is a lounge, if you like, and that way is a magazine shop, and if you hurry, you can play some slots on that far atrium of the airport." Her arms had waved in several directions.

I thanked her and turned toward Liz. I walked over and sat next to her with my knees coupled together. The seating area was sparsely occupied, an elderly couple not far away, a businessman wearing tortoise shell frames buzzing through a copy of the day's news. I opened my hands to her and leaned in. "Liz, I can't answer what you don't tell me about." She said nothing, her first day's courtroom outfit back on. She looked nice, professional, somebody's accountant or sales rep returning home from a business trip.

She shook her head and looked at me, her lips knotted with disgust. "You don't know, Gary? You *don't* know? Well, your attorney's right. You are stupid."

I rolled my eyes and the marshal's words rang in my mind. "Uh, just tell me already."

"You stole our money, and you got Robin pregnant. If that's not enough to end it, I don't know what is. Look, I told myself that you'd show up here and just lie your way out of it, just like you always have."

"I didn't lie to you, and I'm not lying now."

She folded her arms. "I called my dad from the women's jail. I told him what happened at the court today."

"And?"

She made an apologetic face. "And when I get back to Akron, I'm loading up my things, and I'm driving home to California. He offered to wire me money, but I told him that I still had some, that one bundle of tens. That's mine. I'm taking it, and so help me, you just try to stop me. Where's your seat?" she demanded.

"Seat?"

"On the plane," she said, snatching the fluttering ticket copies. "Good, you're not even close to me. And this cab ticket? Don't even try. I'm taking a separate ride from you back to the apartment."

"Aw, don't be like this," I begged. I saw the old man eyeing me, my hands folded in a supplicant's weave.

Liz rolled her eyes. "You got to be kidding me. 'Don't be like this'? Just tell me one thing I've been trying to figure out." Her lips trembled, and I went to rub her back but caught an elbow in return. The old man was whispering to the lady, who glanced over and grinned up at him.

For the first time since the prosecutor mentioned my wife being pregnant, Liz looked me in the eyes, her own tear ducts full. "When did you guys do it? That day you met at Annabelle's? That was it, wasn't it? Just tell me. Be decent about it for God's sake and tell the truth for once!"

I leaned in and hissed, "Please keep your voice down. These people are watching us."

"Good!" she shouted. "Because I don't give a damn." Her lips had that curled edge from the morning at the Courtyard when she convinced me that she hated my guts, that I'd never see her again.

"Liz," I began, my voice an octave lower, "calm down."

"And don't tell me to calm down, damn you! You stole sixty thousand dollars from me!" The old woman heard every syllable and her eyes lit up. "And you fucked your ex-wife, too! Ask him about that," she sobbed, turning toward the old couple.

I stood up. "I'm not making this public. You want the truth, I'll tell you. Otherwise, I'm going down to the concourse to have a drink."

Liz snarled at me and slammed down the flight magazine. "What, so you can think up the next lie?"

I had heard enough. I left.

CHAPTER SEVENTEEN

The greasy-haired chauffeur who met us at the gate in Cleveland listened to Liz and her demands for separate cabs for a full minute. She demanded in a feisty voice that we not ride together.

But he just shook his head. "Me get this straight," he grinned a gray smile. A McDonald's coffee cup fitted into his palm, an extension of his hand. "You want me to tell my boss that I had two fares—both on vouchers, both going to the exact same address—but needed to make two full round-trips from here to Akron all because you're mad at your boyfriend here?" He scoffed and blew air between his lips. "Ain't happening, lady," he said, shaking his head.

Liz puckered her lips while I hung back from the counter. The three-hour flight had been accomplished with me staring at the back of her head, eleven rows ahead. Her one trip to the bathroom went without so much as *boo* between us. "I'll give you a tip—a good one," she insisted.

He jingled his keys, ready to push off. "Lady, I don't care if you give me a thousand dollar-tip, that van out there's taking one trip to Akron tonight, and it's now."

"Okay," she said, "you want to be difficult? A thousand it is."

Undaunted, he walked through the door laughing with me at his side, Liz following. I imagined little plumes of fiery smoke coming through her ears. In the van I rode up front with him while she took the farthest of the bench seats in the rear. He put on easy-listening jazz, she simmered down, and between us the driver and I talked Browns football. By the time we'd made Highland Square, it was dark. Liz slapped a quarter in his palm and muttered something about doing what the customer wants. I had a little cash from my jailhouse discharge and shoved in his hand a wad of ones.

"What'd you do to make 'er sore?" he asked as I hoisted my bag and she went into the building.

"Don't ask, man. You know when people say, 'it's a long story'? Well, this one could be a book, and I'm not lying." He snorted and started for his driver's seat. As he stepped up from the sidewalk, I assured him that I'd do anything for her, and that was the weird part. He swung up into the van, gave me a thumbs up, and roared off into the black Akron night.

* * *

Liz had her bags open, half of them packed, when I came through the door. She threw up a hand at me. "Stop right there! I'm leaving you tonight. We're not going to argue this. If you argue it, I swear I'll have Akron police here so fast it'll make your head spin. I just need some space and an hour, and I will be gone. So, I'm asking you to go across the street—go to the bar if you want. I don't give a shit what you do. I don't. Just don't stay here."

I unfolded my hands and played dumb, hoping it might soften her. "I don't have any money left, plus I got to pay the attorney and the government now. What about that?"

Exasperated, she marched into the next room where I could hear her rustling as I stood listening. Her feet tramped toward me and she appeared. "Here!" she said, waving several bills at me with a slap into my palm. "That's sixty. Go get drunk! Just leave me alone!" Her cheeks burned with color.

I jumped from the top steps outside to the sidewalk, kicking along angry and hopeless. She said an hour, so I figured half that. Sit and think, and yes, maybe have a quick beer while I pondered something.

Crossing the street, I knew that Carrie the barmaid would be working the Bucket Shop. I'd explain it, maybe reconcile with Carrie what had gone on that crazy night. She deserved an apology, too. I realized when she'd threatened to call the police, she'd been appealing to the crowd. I could go there now, have a drink, and maybe get a woman's perspective on the whole mess.

I stomped along the street, crossed over, and swung open the door. Nobody. I planted myself along the main barrier, several seats away from a sitting drink and napkin, a check before it. A man I'd never seen before came from the back, which was fine with me. I ordered rum and Coke and sat down, wishing that the dark-haired, dancing barmaid was on the clock.

Robin Whitehall came out of the ladies restroom.

Robin.

Her appearance startled me, a ghost you've committed words to, never believing in them. I thought of my girlfriend's suggestion that I go drink. Had she known something? Was this whole thing a set up between her and Robin? *Everybody knows everything but me.*

She froze on her way back to the bar as the barkeep set the cocktail before me.

"Robin?"

"What the hell? What are you doing here?" she rambled, her lip mangled with ugliness, her face already working at full drunk.

I shook my head. "Always with the nice language," I said.

"Gary—why are you here?" she said in a demanding way, as though I owed her an apology for having a drink. Off she went to her stool.

I took a good gulp of the rum. The buzz hit me fast, especially after two months of stone sobriety. "Why am I here? Why are you here? And more to the point, why the hell are you drinking when you're pregnant?" The barkeep had disappeared and our voices bounced off the worn and wooden walls.

She threw her head back and roared with laughter, slapping her leg over and over. "Pregnant? You thought I was pregnant? Ah, ha ha ha! You are so stupid sometimes."

I took my drink and moved toward her. "So, you're not?"

"No, I'm not pregnant. Shit. I told them that just to get you in trouble after all you did!"

The rum poured into me and I drank it like 3.2 beer. I shook my head and leaned in and tipped my eyes toward the ceiling. "You're too much, you know that?"

Her face stole a long, telling look across the bar. "You used to think that."

"Hey, a toast," I announced, raising what was left of the cocktail. She joined me. "Here's to you not being pregnant."

"I guess," she deadpanned, clinking her glass to mine.

"Whew, that is a load off. And you know what else, dear wife of mine? You know . . . I got an idea." I was close now, a suggestive distance from her lips. My eyes were fixed on the painted lips, how they glistened with life, the nerve that drove the woman who lied through them, poured endless drinks over them, and satisfied a circuit of lovers with them. "Ever hear someone say 'can't beat 'em, join 'em'?"

She dipped her chin tentatively.

I leaned in and whispered, "I've been thinking about getting naked with you for a long time, lots of lonely nights in jail." I pointed at the door. "I got a place across the street that's available. What do you say? Let's go. It'll be fun."

"You serious?"

"Yeah, who's gonna know? Besides," I said, scrunching my lips, "we're husband and wife. Law says we're allowed to have sex anytime we want."

She tweaked her nose at me, eyes cockeyed. "I didn't think about it like that. You're right."

"I'm serious," I laughed, "don't you remember the last time we were here, this very spot? I mean, you said it right in my ear, didn't you? That you wanted to go to bed? Well, this is a good time for it." I patted my pants pocket. "Let me pay you out." I dipped my head with a shake, raising my eyebrows as I peeled off bills. "But I'll warn you, I might be a little rough with you. It's been a while."

Her eyes lit into little flames, and she began caressing my chest. "Hmm, that might be nice. I've missed this, you know?"

I turned to the far doorway. "Hey in there. Can we cash out?"

The same man breezed toward us and told me I owed fourteen and change between the two tabs. I peeled off one of the twenties and kissed Robin hard in front of him, hard enough where she protested.

"Hey, that hurt!" That wicked smile of hers appeared like a snake from summer weeds and through the bar's door we went, hand in hand. Halfway across the street, her hand became a revulsion to me, its alcohol clamminess. I hated her. But I kept nuzzling, bumping, and grabbing her ass with my good hand. Traffic had died in the street. Akron looked lonely.

Up the steps we went, Robin giggling, splashing her feet here and there, leaning on me as though we were about to fall onto some silent mattress so she could relive a twisted fantasy. When I turned the door handle to our apartment, I swung Robin across the threshold just as Liz was coming out of the kitchen area, a cleaning rag in her hand. She froze, eyes wide, fixing them on me, then on my wife.

"Whoa!" Robin shouted, astonished and sobered all at once.

"Gary!" Liz cried.

I dug my fingers into Robin's arm. "Now both of you! Hold it and listen! We're going to get the truth right now." I lifted Robin so hard one of her feet cleared the floor. "She's got something to say here." I glared at Robin. "Now, go ahead. Tell her what you just told me over there!"   •

She grimaced at my grip. "You're hurting me."

"I don't give a shit. Tell the truth!" I felt my face and neck go purple.

Robin faltered, her eyes like a blind woman's. "I'm not pregnant," she muttered. "Just made it up to get even."

Liz soured her face. "So, you two screwed and she didn't get pregnant. Big deal."

"Tell her, Robin. So help me, you better tell her," I said, tightening my grip even more.

"We never . . . you know, did it. He only gave me a ride home because I needed one. Nothing happened." She sounded disappointed.

"You—you wait here," I shouted. I marched through the apartment to my little dresser and snatched up the business card.

I heard Robin address Liz. "You got a nice place here."

"Well, I'm leaving anyways," Liz said. "So I hope you're happy."

I walked back in and stared Liz down in the light. "Okay, Miss Robin," I began, handing her the card, "on Monday, I want you to call this guy. The divorce is on me. I'll pay, but we are getting a divorce, so you know."

She looked at it and wobbled at first but piped up with a shrug. "Just as well. Derek's been on me to file. My dad's been on me, too. In fact, he's already got the attorney who has some papers drawn up. I'll sign," she said, her eyes glassy with tears. "I just wish that—"

"No," I announced, opening the door. "It is over. Final. Get the thing going. I love Liz here, only she don't know it." I waved my hand at Liz with disgusted lips, angrier than I had been for a long time, since Stanley had tried to murder us. Liz stood perfectly still, watching me. "And now, I'll ask you to leave and wish you well with getting some help. That's all I can offer. I've been through a lot because of you, so pardon me if I don't kiss your ass. Those days are over." I backed her out of the place, her wounded eyes the last thing I saw as I closed the door.

CHAPTER EIGHTEEN

The following morning, blue jays woke me up with their screaming. I considered coffee but fell back into the pillow instead, exhausted from the night before. Last night had turned to right now. I pulled myself up, reluctant to leave a soft bed where I could sleep. Liz was out cold on the sofa, a tall blanket resting high over her face. I reached for the phone and called Buddy.

When she woke and we left in the car, Liz was guarded, not saying much. I couldn't make her trust me, and as we wound through the stark plains south of Akron, rolling through soft hills that turned steep and wooded, we talked. Where were we going, she wanted to know.

I just kept driving, farther and farther south, then west and then, with one great departure, we whirred from the interstate and down a myriad of hills and turns, all two-laners flanked by occasional filling stations and general stores with gravel parking lots. Winding, turning, not offering a word to one another. I'd not given her a syllable of a hint about where we were headed.

The whir of air through the car drove me crazy as we roared down the country bi-way. "I have a good surprise."

"What are you talking about?"

I lifted my hand. "I want it to be good, I want it right. Every blessed thing in California was wrong for me. Except you. I paid a high price to be here."

For the first time, she looked over at me, peeling a single strand of hair from the corner of her mouth as the air continued through the car.

"I'm not done. I'd do it again—the murders, jail, divorce—if I had to, just to be with you. That's all I'm saying. And that's all you need to hear, for now."

"Where are you taking me?"

"Just hear me out for a second. You can say whatever you want, but the first time I had you in my arms at that bakery I was in love. I had no right to be but I was."

The roads were enveloped with low hanging trees, shading the road in freckles, and I breathed out. We turned off the state route toward the magical road and country lane. I turned toward her. "And while you tell me how you don't believe anything I say, mark this moment in time: I brought you here to live in this place in 1990." The car rumbled up the gravel road, a gentle but definite grade to where the holler breezes shook the lowest boughs. They wore a dusting of brown powder from the lane.

"This is it," I said, turning upward through the trees. In the distance I saw booted feet coming, a man's legs.

She grasped my arm. "Who's that coming?"

I laughed and saw through a clearing of fine waving grasses. "That's Buddy." And he walked with great intent, a coarse beard set down in his chest. Before him he carried a wicker basket brimming with strawberries. He came at us and I slowed, then stopped while the road dust covered the car. I rolled down the window, coughing. "Hey, Buddy Ray, what's going on?"

"Got some berries for you, sweet ones," he said. He leaned down and handed me the basket that I in turn set in Leslie's lap. "This the lady you told me about?" His eyes twinkled like a storybook character's, and Liz smiled with him. "Ma'am, I'll tell you right now. This fellow here, he goes for you."

"Well," she said, "I guess I go for him, too."

Buddy stood up, towering over the car, and waved to some distant point. "You can go on up there and park. Let her see the place. We got a whole dinner my wife's setting out for tonight. A roast and all the extras." He motioned me on as the blue car hummed up the hill to where the cabin stood.

As I pulled up, Liz paused, her mouth hesitant. "Gary, what is this place?"

"All the money you thought was stolen, it's here. This place is what I couldn't tell you about when I was in handcuffs. This place is yours, Liz. It's all yours. Just wait till you see the views."

Made in the USA
Middletown, DE
20 December 2015